A Husband for Matilda

A
Husband for
Matilda

E. Ayers

A Husband for Matilda
By E. Ayers
First Print Edition
copyright © 2020
All rights reserved.
ISBN-13: 978-1-62522-000-0
March 2020

This literary work is independently published by the author in association with Indie Artist Press. If you receive this book in print format without a cover, or electronically by any means other than purchase through established channels or participation in a bona-fide ebook sharing subscription or program, the author did not receive compensation. Piracy of electronic or printed literary works is a crime.

All rights reserved. This book or any portion thereof may not be reproduced or used in any manner whatsoever without the express written permission of the author or publisher except for the use of brief quotations in critical articles or reviews.

This is a work of fiction. Names, places, businesses, characters, and incidents are either the product of the author's imagination or are used in a fictitious manner. Any resemblance to actual persons living or dead, actual events, or locales is purely coincidental.

For George, who believed in me

ONE

Matilda Berwyn waited until her father and brother left the tiny abode where they lived. Still wearing her nightshirt, she washed the cups, bowls, and spoons they had used for breakfast. She was anxious to retrieve the page from a newspaper that she had carefully hidden between several pieces of split wood by the door of their soddy. She had tucked it there before her family had returned from Mr. Van Dyke's copper mine. Now that page weighed on her.

She loved to read, but her father had no books, not even a Bible. Buying a piece of meat wrapped in a newspaper was heavenly. Last night's fish came wrapped in two pages of news from the Chicago Tribune. That was a real treat. She had unwrapped the fish and carefully folded the newspaper, praying the entire time that the pages wouldn't stick together.

With the men gone from the house, she yanked off her nightshirt and found her pants and shirt. She took a clean roll of cloth strips and began her daily chore of binding her breasts. Living in a mining camp could be dangerous for a female, and she knew it. When they'd moved to Homestead Canyon, her father lied about her age and claimed she was a boy. He swore it was safer for her. He had taken his knife and lopped off her hair that had hung below her waist, leaving her with carrot-colored curls to frame her face. Several times her father attempted to cut it shorter and each time, she cried and begged him not to do it. It seemed the shorter it was the curlier it was. Her attempt to run the comb through her knotted corkscrews left her on the verge of tears. She hated her hair.

She pulled the shirt over her head and tied it at her neck, certain the shirt had once been white, but now it was beige. The pants she pulled on were probably two sizes too big. She rolled the bottoms, threaded a length of rope through the loops, and tied that at her waist. Then she gathered all the dirty clothing and tied it into her father's shirt to take for washing in the creek.

A quick gaze around the their home told her all was well. Leaving the bundle of clothes by the stove, she opened the door and retrieved the newspaper. Breathing a sigh of relief, she unfolded the pages. A quick scan and she found the word. *In…di…gen…ous.*

She huffed and refolded the paper, returning it to its hiding place. The sun still hadn't crept above the horizon, but the day promised to be another clear and bright one. As she walked through the tent town and towards Mr. Van Dyke's house in Homestead Canyon, she wondered if someday she could write articles for a newspaper. She remembered her teacher in California talking about women working. *Oh, to have my own money.* The thought of wearing a fancy dress and pretty shoes with lots of buttons made her heart skip a beat. *A dark green one, the color of the fir trees by the river and a colorful shawl that I can drape around my shoulders.* She sighed. Her thoughts turned to marriage. *Somebody wealthy such as Mr. Van Dyke with a pretty house… Mmm. Won't happen. Pa, will soon start telling folks I'm addled.*

The town was practically empty as the men were working at the mine. But there was some activity on the street and the dust from a passing cart almost choked her. They needed rain. Mr. Jones swept the porch of the company store. And she wondered why, because it would be dusty in less than an hour.

She saw Mr. Van Dyke on his steed and silently said a prayer that he wouldn't ask her to run an errand this morning. There was only one thing she wanted and that was to use Miz Rosalind Van Dyke's dictionary.

"Morning, Matt." Mr. Van Dyke raised his hand in a wave and headed off in the direction of the mine.

She broke in a full run towards his house and then flew up the steps to the front door. She lifted the brass knocker and let it fall against the plate with a loud bang. Then she listened for sound inside the house. Hearing none, she repeated her knock, almost cringing at the sharp noise.

"Coming!" The door opened. "Good morning, Matt. Mr. Van Dyke just left, and he said nothing to me about needing you today."

"Yes, Miz Rosalind. I just saw him." Suddenly her mouth went dry. "I-I… I came to see you. I want to use your dictionary. I found a word."

"Oh, Matt. I think it's wonderful that you are always looking to learn new words. Mr. Van Dyke said you had finished your schooling before coming here."

Matilda nodded. *Another of my pa's lies.*

"If you hadn't, my husband would have been forced to provide a teacher for you. Most of the children in town aren't quite old enough for school." She motioned for Matilda to follow her. "Maybe next year he will bring a teacher to Homestead Canyon."

Matilda followed the woman through the house to a room with shelves. The last time she had visited the room there were hardly any books, but now there were quite a few. She rubbed her fingers together. She wanted to touch each one, to open them, and read them. Like forbidden fruit, they called to her.

Miz Rosalind removed a fat book and placed it on a table. "Let me see your hands, Matt. I know boys don't like washing their hands, but I don't want dirty fingerprints on my books."

Matilda held up her hands. "I just washed the dishes. They are clean."

Miz Rosalind took Matilda's hands and inspected them.

"Yes, they are clean, Matt. I'm very proud of you. You're a good boy. Even your nails are clean and neatly trimmed."

"Thanks. My ma said God's children were supposed to be clean. He wants to be proud of us."

"Your mother was a smart woman."

"Thank you. I miss her." Matilda opened the book where the little divot displayed 'I'. Then she moved a few pages to "ind" and found the word. She sounded out the word. "Indigenous."

Matilda lingered over the word, read a few more words on the page and tried to memorize every new one that she saw. But Miz Rosalind's gaze felt as though it was boring into Matilda's back, and she knew not to linger. "Thank you, ma'am. You look mighty pretty in that yellow dress."

"Thank you, Matt. Are you done?"

"Yes, Miz Rosalind." She tried not to chew at her lip and followed the woman to the front door.

A sweet, floral scent lingered around Mr. Van Dyke's wife, and the dress she wore swished with her every move. Matilda yearned to be able to wear such a dress and to be an important lady with many books.

As she stepped across the threshold, Miz Rosalind asked, "Do you own a pair of boots?"

Matilda pulled her back ramrod straight. "Yes, ma'am. I'd just rather run barefooted when the weather is warm."

"That's fine. Sometimes I think I'd rather run barefooted, too."

Without turning around, Matilda raised her hand in a wave, and called thanks as she took off in a full run for the family soddy. Now that she understood the word, she wanted to reread the article.

A half hour later, Matilda stood in the stream that ran behind the soddy, washed the family's clothes, and then draped them over bushes to dry. She thought about visiting Mrs. Ella Watson and borrowing another book. Ella had lots of books, including ones on history and even some on mathematics. About once a month, the company store would have something for Matilda to deliver to their place and she enjoyed the long walk to the Watson Ranch. But the last time she was there, Mrs. Ella Watson wasn't, so Matilda returned the book she had borrowed and didn't have one to bring home.

Her mind wandered back in time. When her father discovered Mr. Van Dyke was bringing a stamp mill to Wyoming, he packed up and followed the mill, knowing that a stamp mill would be used for copper or gold, and it didn't matter to him which one it was. Her father was a miner. He had grand dreams, but all he ever did was work in a mine. She remembered when they arrived. There was nothing but a handful of tents and covered wagons. The town consisted of about twenty people, and she was the only female. She'd watched Homestead Canyon grow and watched as Mr. Van Dyke built his big house. *I want a big house.*

The sound of an owl grabbed her attention. She called back to it and the owl answered her call.

A smile tugged at her cheeks. Gray Fox was her childhood friend and the perfect diversion for another hot day in Homestead Canyon. His dark hair was cut to his shoulders and he only wore a loincloth made of soft leather. His tribe refused to stay on a reservation and maintained their nomadic lifestyle. His big smile and dimples had endeared him to her when they first met.

He appeared and held out a pouch filled with berries.

"Where did you find them?" She followed her young friend to a thicket. But before she started to pick berries, Gray Fox handed her a package. In it were corncakes that had been soaked in honey. The treat was delightful and topping it off with freshly picked, sweet berries was heavenly.

After they had eaten, Gray Fox produced a handful of round clay balls and they played as they chatted in the cool shade of some trees.

Zeke Hillerman stood before Arnold Haas and listened carefully to the man's directives. Zeke knew he was lucky to have such a man as a boss. Mr. Haas didn't just give orders; he explained things.

Zeke had grown up on a farm outside of Germantown, Pennsylvania. He knew how to raise cattle, care for horses, and grow vegetables. His parents were self-sufficient. But he wanted more than a small farm on the outskirts of Philadelphia. He wanted the world at his fingertips. And people like Arnold Haas were teaching him how. But he needed money for his dreams and this job paid well.

"Yes, sir." Zeke smiled as he responded. "I'll catch a nap and leave tonight. I'll take Shep with me."

"Good idea. Shep's a good dog. You've trained him well."

Eight hours later, it was dark as Zeke prepared to leave the stockyard with four steers and two mules for delivery in

Homestead Canyon. The primitive map didn't give him much other than a few landmarks. If he followed the railroad, the trip would be longer but easier. Mr. Haas suggested that Zeke take the northern route around the two mountains, and then warned him that a few tribes used that land for hunting.

Zeke knew the responsibility of moving a few head of cattle was heavy, especially alone, but doing it through Indian hunting grounds sent a shiver through his system. He said a prayer that he'd avoid the Indians on this drive to Homestead Canyon. Gently, he nudged his horse forward and called to Shep. He had plenty of food in tins to keep him well fed during his travels. With luck, he'd be there before sunset. He'd sleep for a few hours and then come back.

The drive through the night went smoothly with only a small amount of protesting from the steers. But as dawn broke, Zeke realized how far he'd come and how alone he was with the animals. Light turned dark columns into deep green fir trees that were surrounded by jade green grasses, with tuffs of gray-green plants poking through the grass in places. It was beautiful, but he focused his attention on the path in front of him. He had a rocky steep climb. He took the animals to a tiny, but swift creek, and let them drink and nibble on the tall grass while he opened a tin and had some breakfast.

As he ate his muffin, he surveyed the terrain and tossed Shep a few strips of jerky. Getting the cattle up that steep rocky hill would take skill. Zeke pulled out his map and looked it over carefully. Worrying about the trail wasn't going to make the drive any easier. He called to the dog and started on the last leg of his journey.

The horse and mules made their way to the top of the rise, but the cattle were slower and not quite as sure-footed. Shep barked and kept them moving forward. The plaintive moos told Zeke that they had enough intelligence to know they were in danger of falling. But soon all the animals had joined him. That's when he looked at the valley before him. It was a real beauty, all green and lush.

Someplace, probably off to his right, was the copper mine. He'd made excellent time. He nudged his horse and rode down the gentle slope, into the narrow valley below. He traversed to the far side of the valley and rode up the gentle slope. The top of the slight rise gave him a view of Homestead Canyon to his right, but almost out of sight, he spotted a young boy bent over the water. Partially obscured by trees, Zeke couldn't tell what the child was doing, alone, in the middle of nowhere. But it was impossible to miss the fact that the child had hair the color of polished copper.

By the time Zeke made it to his destination, he was tired. Every part of his body ached and as soon as the man at the livery signed the paperwork, Zeke found a shaded area and slept for a few hours. He awakened slightly disoriented and then remembered where he was. After rummaging around in his saddlebags, he found more tins of food. One contained sausages and pickled cabbage. He devoured the contents and went looking for more to eat. Two fluffy rolls had been cut open and slathered with butter and another tin contained a pastry filled with a sweet cream. The one remaining tin had more rolls filled with salty ham.

He looked around the quiet town and found a well pump, where he filled his canteen. After washing his hands and face, he cupped his hands and slurped plenty of cold water. He was ready for the ride home.

From this side, he had no clue where he had crossed the other range. Twice he rode between the mountains only to discover an impossible path, but the third time he discovered rocky but easy to navigate terrain that would put him back on the way to the Haas'. He pulled out his map and marked it as he ate the last of his food. He'd gone too far north the first time. This was the better place to cross between the mountains.

Matilda fixed a dinner with beans, carrots, and potatoes. She had picked and then pickled some fiddleheads from some ferns along the stream. While she waited for the meal to cook, she mended her brother's pants. Her mind wandered to Rosalind and some of the other women she'd seen in town in their long dresses. Those women were pretty and curvy, and their hair was pulled up. They acted so lady-like. Even the way they walked was different. Mattie looked at her hands. *Freckles. Millions of freckles.*

Sometimes she'd catch her reflection in a window and that thought made her sigh. *I don't really look like a boy.* Too skinny, short, and scrawny to be a boy, she knew she was ugly. It was as though a great weight descended on her shoulders. She ran her needle under several stitches and tied off the thread that she had used to patch her brother's pants.

After she stirred the pot, she wandered into the soddy and put her needle and thread into the tiny box that she kept on a shelf. She could hear her father and brother returning from the mine. Her brother was cursing and her father sounded angry. There was no question that she was in for a horrible evening if they were in a bad mood.

She gathered three bowls and took them outside to where the tiny Franklin stove stood in a clearing. It made more sense to put the stove outside during the hot summer months rather than heat up the tiny house where they lived. She wondered where Rosalind made meals because she'd never seen a kitchen in the house. But on several occasions Mattie had followed Gray Fox to the encampment where he lived with his family and those women made meals in the center of their tents. Except that rising heat seemed to drag in the outside air and cool the tent.

Earlier, Gray Fox had caught a young rabbit and taken it home to his family. He would be dining on that tonight. She had tasted rabbit once and thought it was delicious. But everything Gray Fox's mom made was delicious. She would miss him. He told her his family was moving tomorrow to another spot.

She filled the bowls and returned to the soddy. "Hi, Pa."

"Why are you actin' so cheerful? Maybe because while we're workin', yous sittin' doin' nuttin' except readin' another book?"

"I found some fiddleheads and pickled them. I know they are a favorite of yours."

Her father didn't answer her. Instead, he turned to her brother and began to complain about the day. From what she gathered, something had gone wrong, which slowed production. She knew her father was probably the most experienced miner in Homestead Canyon. He'd spent years coal mining before going to California and he swore Van Dyke didn't cheat the men like some of the other mine owners. But whatever had happened today was sitting on him like soured milk. She prayed he didn't take out his frustration on her. The one thing she hated more than anything was listening to him rant and complain, especially when it was directed at her.

The following morning, when the sun rose, Matilda followed the stream to her favorite spot where trees shaded the water. Taking her pan, she began to look for gold. Some days, she could pan all day and find nothing; others would yield a few flakes, and today was promising, as a thunderstorm had raged someplace nearby for she had heard the deep rumbles, but the storm had failed to send a drop into Homestead Canyon. The stream, that normally only trickled in this section, flowed swiftly from last night's rain. With one hand she stirred the pebbles from the creek bed while she swirled the muddy debris through her pan. As her hand collected the pebbles, she spotted it - a nugget, the size of her palm. She dove for it, missed, and dove again. Her whole body shook as she held it. Never had she seen such a large chunk. Furiously, she worked for hours, under the blazing sun, and when she finally gave up she had the one large nugget and several smaller ones. Never had she found so much gold in a single day. She was far from the mine. Mr. Van Dyke couldn't claim it was his or accuse her of stealing. Placing the nuggets in her wooden box, she buried the box in her hiding spot and made it home before her family would return looking for their meal.

She had promised herself when the box was filled, she would leave Homestead Canyon. Except now the box was almost filled. She wanted nothing more than to buy a dress and some fancy shoes. *Certainly that will make me a lady.* Then she'd seek a job as a newspaper reporter or as a novelist and live in a pretty house.

Zeke was now accustomed to making the drive to Homestead Canyon. Every few weeks, he'd drive a few head of cattle to the mining town. It was something he began to look forward to doing. It was like taking a holiday from his regular chores. He knew the route well and had never once encountered an Indian. For him, it was an easy drive. Alone with his thoughts, he'd dream of what he wanted. And learning the stockyard end of ranching was valuable information.

He made his way through the mountain passes and surveyed the land before him. The sun beat down on him causing him to wipe the sweat from his face. Movement caught his attention and he watched. It didn't take him a second to recognize the redheaded child that he often saw along the stream.

He watched as this young person pulled an old shirt off and then began to unwrap material from the body. *Oh, dear God, it's a woman!* Part of him said not to watch but another part of him was fascinated. She stripped down to nothing and then stepped into the water. It was obvious that she was bathing. His body warmed to the point that he thought it might combust, and it wasn't from the sun that beat on his shoulders.

He wanted to move closer to see more, but he was riveted in place by two steers and a dog. Never before had he seen a woman naked and she was a beauty. Now he understood the stirrings he'd had since crossing into manhood. He shifted in his saddle in an attempt to relieve the pressure building in him.

Slowly, she rose from the water and walked to dry land. She tossed her head sending her copper colored curls in motion and ran her fingers through them. Then she ran her hands over her body as though she was pushing water off of it. Zeke groaned. Standing on her tiptoes, she stretched. A moment later, she began to gather her clothes and wrap the strips of cloth around her body. Soon she was dressed like a young boy.

Why?

Still awestruck, he watched as she vanished into the woods. When he decided to move, she emerged and began to do something in a narrow section of that stream. He'd heard of people panning for gold but he'd never seen anyone actually attempting to do it. Yet he was certain that's what she was doing.

Shep became restless. Not wanting the dog to bark and give away their vantage point, Zeke continued his journey into Homestead Canyon.

Mr. Van Dyke met Zeke as he rode through town.

Zeke had pictured an older man, but Mr. Van Dyke was fairly young. Still, Zeke greeted Mr. Van Dyke as though the man were an old, wise sage.

"How do you run them here so fast?" Mr. Van Dyke asked.

Zeke smiled at the man. "I don't ride them hard - just keep them moving. I couldn't do it without the help of Shep." He pointed to his dog. "I leave at night and we don't stop. Give them a day or two with some fresh grass, and they'll be as tender as can be."

"Does Haas deal in pigs?"

Zeke chuckled. "If it has four feet, he'll find it."

"I was wondering about buying a male hog and letting him roam free."

Zeke shook his head. "Gotta keep him penned. Three weeks of freedom and a hog will turn into a wild boar."

"Three weeks?"

"Yes, sir. They have to be treated like pets."

Mr. Van Dyke nodded.

"Mr. Haas has a supplier for chicken, layer or roasters, but he won't ship them in the summer or in the winter, just spring and fall. He guarantees satisfaction."

"Hmm. I'll keep that in mind. We could use both around here."

"He also ships turkey, quail, and doves."

Mr. Van Dyke nodded. "I enjoy hunting once in a while, but I think the town might enjoy a feast this fall. I'll keep it in mind."

"Yes, sir. Let Mr. Haas know. He'll ship directly to Hanover. I'll meet them at the train and bring them up."

Mr. Van Dyke started to ride off, but Zeke wanted an answer to a burning question. "Sir, there's a young boy around here…red hair—"

"Matt. He's the young son of one of my miners. Good boy. He runs errands for me occasionally. Is there a problem?"

"No, not at all. I see him once in a while." Zeke raised his hand in a wave and took off for the livery where he delivered the steers. *Matt? He's no boy.*

After the steers were delivered, Zeke headed for the rise behind the mine. He wanted to see Matt one more time before returning to the Haas stockyard.

Matilda couldn't wait to return to that spot in the stream. She'd found more gold yesterday than she had in weeks of panning. With care, she had managed to lift a few stones and find a few nuggets. Most weren't any bigger than her thumbnail and quite a few were the size of a tiny pea, but that was still better than the little flakes she had been finding. Gold was her ticket out of Homestead Canyon, a way to escape her life as a boy.

But before she could pan today, her father said Mr. Van Dyke wanted her to stop at the store and run some errands for Mr. Jones. Normally she would have enjoyed chasing around Homestead Canyon and being given a piece of candy for her efforts, but today she only wanted to go back to that golden spot in the stream.

As soon as she had the soddy clean and neat, she rushed

into town. Mr. Jones was probably her pa's age with a mustache that seemed to wiggle with every word the man spoke. Most of the miners removed their facial hair in the summer, but Mr. Jones had kept his mustache.

"Hey, Matt. I need you to make deliveries this morning."

Matilda smiled up at the man. She liked watching his mustache. "How many?"

"Quite a few." He put his hand on two packages tied with string. "Run this to the saloon and then take this to Mr. Van Dyke's kitchen."

She nodded and took off. Her father didn't like her chatting with the folks who worked at the saloon, but the women who worked there were always nice to her. Except at this hour of the morning, she was certain the women were still sound asleep.

She did all of the errands in record time and then came back for her candy sticks. "Two sassafras."

"Two? I was told to give you one."

"No, two. That was twice the amount of errands than I usually run."

A voice from the back of the store said, "Give him two."

Matilda instantly recognized the voice. "Thank you, Miz Rosalind."

"You're welcome. We appreciate what you do around here."

Matilda took the two proffered sticks and ran out the door. She had taken items from the store to almost every household in Homestead Canyon. Several times she'd been given a penny when she delivered. She stuffed that change into her pocket, knowing she'd add it to her box. *My precious box.*

From the angle of the sun, she knew it was almost midmorning as she headed to the stream. Her pan was hidden under a shrub. She always made certain the metal pan was covered in mud and a layer of moss covered the dirt. Unless someone was looking for a pan, they would never spot it. She had to lie on the ground and reach under the prickly bush to retrieve her pan, but it was safe there. Once she had the pan, she went looking for her box. She knew by the placement of the stones it was still safe.

The box was beginning to weigh a ton. A soft laugh bubbled from her. She didn't realize how much gold weighed until she started to collect it. The box contained a small hammer that she had found. The handle had broken and someone tossed it. She whittled a new handle for it. When the farrier had come to Homestead Canyon, he had tossed a knife that had broken. The tip was useless but the shank was still good. She whittled a new handle for that and had the blacksmith hone it into a useable knife. The blade was merely an inch long and very pointed but it was all she needed to cut flakes from stones. The blacksmith had laughed at her request and then never charged her. He told her she was a silly boy, but he managed to create the sharp edge, and pin the handle to the shank. She had the tools and that gold was her ticket to freedom.

She went back to her favorite spot. Squatting in the cool water, she began to lift stones. She almost screamed with delight when she uncovered a nugget that was almost the size of her two thumbs. *If only I could weigh everything.*

She placed each nugget she found into a pouch until she

filled it. Each one brought her closer to running away, each one would go towards a house someplace far away from Homestead Canyon, and each one would buy her books and fancy dresses.

The sun began to descend into the western sky when she gave up. She'd barely found anything in the last two hours, but that one large nugget made up for everything. She went to her box and uncovered it. The previous storekeeper was going to burn the box, but she had begged him for it. Upon arrival in Homestead Canyon, the box had contained salted codfish, but now it was her secret stash. She slid the cover off the box and added today's gold to it. Then discovered that she couldn't close the lid. She pounded on the gold until it was flattened enough that she could slid the lid onto the box. *I need another box. I need something for supper tonight!*

She stopped at the company store long enough to buy some yellow squash, some fatback, and some cornmeal on her father's tab. "Do you have any more boxes for me?"

"Why do you want boxes, Matt?"

She shrugged. "I don't know. I like them. I like finding stuff, and it keeps things neat."

Roscoe Jones shook his head. "You are a strange boy, Matt." Mr. Jones disappeared to the back of the shop, and then reappeared with two boxes. "I should be charging you for these."

"No. You shouldn't. You are tossing them into the burn pile. I'm doing you a favor by taking them off your hands."

Mr. Jones laughed. "You drive a hard bargain, Matt."

She grinned at the shopkeeper and took off with her treasures. After hiding her boxes behind her pallet, she began to make dinner. She prayed that her father wouldn't be angry if dinner wasn't waiting for him as he walked through the door.

She cut off a slice of fat back and melted it in a pan. Using all the oil she had saved, she sautéed her squash and onions. Then made some cornbread. While the cornbread was cooking, she set the table, knowing that her father would return from the mine hungry. Then she took a tiny twig and stuck it into the center of the cornbread. The stick came out wet but the edges of the cornbread were becoming crunchy. She turned a larger pot over the top of the cornbread pan and prayed that would speed the baking.

In the waning outdoor light, she removed the toes from a pair of socks that had been darned so many times that she was patching patches. Then using the wool from an old red scarf, she crocheted new toes onto the socks. In between crochet stitches, she checked on the cornbread until it was done. Her father was late coming home. That's when she remembered it was payday for the men. She knew where he was - at the saloon, drinking his pay.

She trimmed a tiny sliver from the block of fatback and melted it over the crunchy browned edges of the cornbread and ate them. Then she had a portion of the squash and onions, and cleaned up her plates. She cut up the remaining cornbread and placed it in a glass jar. In another glass jar, she put the squash and onions. Sitting in the greenish-blue glass cast an odd color on the food. She wrinkled her nose, knowing her father would probably turn down the meal and demand that she make something else. She was tired and wanted to go to bed as the sun set behind the mine. But on a payday night, it wasn't a safe thing to do. It was important to her that she stay awake and face whatever her drunken father might dole at her. At least the only thing her brother ever did was tumble into bed and sleep off his drunken stupor. She hoped her father would do the same thing, but she usually didn't get that lucky. It wasn't her fault that her father didn't like his life.

Zeke awakened and stretched. He had found the perfect spot for sleeping. Using his bedroll as a pillow, he'd slept through the night and well into the morning hours, leaving him feeling refreshed and ready for the ride to the Haas stockyard. He scanned the water below and didn't see Matt. Unfortunately, he couldn't wait forever. It was important that he return to the stockyard in a timely manner. But that didn't stop the disappointment that ran through him.

As he prepared to leave, movement caught his eye and he stopped long enough to realize it was Matt. *She's not playing. She really is panning for gold!*

He stood there mesmerized. Whatever she was finding wasn't small. He left his horse and went back down the pass to get a better look. A spear whizzed through the air and landed near Matt.

Zeke instantly stiffened. His rifle was with his backpack, leaving him only with his knife. There was no time to think.

He had to protect Matt. He took off in a full run, his boots barely touching the ground. A blood-curdling yell resonated across the peaceful landscape as an Indian ran towards Matt.

Zeke dove for the young man slamming him into the creek bed. With his fist raised, Zeke looked into two dark orbs that instantly widened…

"Who is he?" Gray Fox asked.

Matilda sat in the creek after she dragged the man from the water and watched him. "Not sure. Think he's going to die?"

"As hard as you hit him with that rock, he might." Gray Fox lifted his shoulders and let them drop. "If he dies, they will say I did it."

"No they won't, because no one will know you were with me."

"You think you have all the answers because you're older than me."

She smiled at her friend. "Yes, I am older, and I can read and write. You need to learn."

"I can speak your language."

Matilda blew out a breath. "Yes, as I have learned yours, but you need to read and write. You need to go to school."

Gray Fox shook his head.

The man moaned.

Gray Fox stood and handed her his knife. "Take it. You might need it. I think he was after me, not you. But in case I'm wrong, my knife is much better than that tiny thing you carry."

Matilda took the knife and watched Gray Fox move away.

The man moaned again, and this time she could see that blood flowed from the back of his head where she had hit him. Very quickly, she hid her gold and her pan. *If I hurry… I can do this… must.*

She raced home. Every breath of air felt like fire in her chest. She gathered a few strips of material, and her needle and thread. As she was leaving the soddy, the cornbread caught her eye. She put two pieces in her pocket and took off.

The man was still lying by the creek.

She rolled him over and inspected the gash. Red and white with bits of clotting, there were areas that were still seeping blood. Around the gash was blond hair that was matted in clotted blood. The shaking in her hands matched the shaking in her stomach. She knew her own breathing had to return to normal before she could help him. Cupping some water in her hand, she poured it over his wound. He groaned and went totally limp.

She jumped back and waited to see if he was still breathing. Assured that he was, she went to work, creating one crossed stitch to close the gash. She soaked one strip of material in the water and folded it onto itself and then she used another strip to hold the wet pad against his head. Now she had to wait.

Minutes seemed like hours, and occasionally Gray Fox would let her know he was nearby with his owl call. The man lying before her was handsome. He had the stubble of whiskers that matched the blond color of his hair. His skin was smooth without pocks or scars. Two tidy eyebrows arched over his eyes and accentuated a strong, straight nose. *He's handsome and even his clothes appear to belong to someone who's been well tended. What have I done?*

Shortly after she heard the noonday whistle at the mine blow, Gray Fox appeared with a handful of sweet berries. It was a wonderful treat and Matilda gobbled most of them up and then felt guilty. She saved a few for the wounded man.

Gray Fox called to her.

She slipped away and found her friend.

"How's he doing?"

"I must have hit him harder than I thought I did. But how am I supposed to know how hard to hit him?"

Gray Fox shook his head. "I found his horse and his dog. The dog won't let me near the horse."

"Oh, was that the barking I heard?"

Gray Fox nodded and dug in his pouch. "Here's a bit of tree bark. If his bleeding has stopped, you can give him some of this. We make a tea with it."

"This is willow. But I have no way to know how much to give him. I am not a doctor." She looked at the strip of bark in her hand. "I can soak it in the water and see if he will suck on it."

Gray Fox shook his head and went away.

She wanted to look for nuggets, not spend her day staring at a stranger, even if he was a fine-looking man. She watched the man move slightly before moaning. Certain he was waking up, she braced for whatever might happen next.

Zeke's head pounded as his eyes fluttered opened and he tried to focus. *Water?* He searched his memory and then remembered the Indian. Trying to get a better view of his surroundings, he moved his head and thought it might explode with pain. The sun hurt his eyes. He remembered looking into the young man's eyes. He was just a kid, probably not more than twelve years old. Nothing beyond that came to his mind. Well, maybe just the memory of pain.

He flexed his fingers and moved his feet. Nothing hurt other than his head. Lifting his hand to run his fingers through his hair, he realized he had a bandage.

"Hey, you gonna live?"

The sound of rustling stopped and he slowly opened his eyes. It was Matt. Her eyes were as green as the leaves on the trees and her face was covered in a million freckles. "What happened? I was trying to protect you and suddenly the lights went out."

"Protect me? From what?"

"From that Indian."

Matt laughed. "He's my friend. Just don't tell anyone. I've even been to his camp, met his ma and pa. My pa would put his belt to my hide if he knew."

She moved away, letting the sun beat down on him, so he shielded his eyes from the light.

"He's Lakota. They are dangerous."

"No, he's not. He's my friend."

"He was going to attack you." He pulled himself into a sitting position. His head throbbed louder than that horrible pounding sound that came from the mine.

"He likes to try to scare me, but I knew he was coming. I saw him coming down the hill."

"Is this water any good for drinking?"

Matt shrugged. "Probably won't kill you. I'll bring you better water. There's a spring over there."

He watched as she scampered away. She was covered in freckles, giving her a burnished look to otherwise milky-white skin. *Adorable*.

She returned with a metal cup filled with cold water and handed it to him.

"Thanks. I needed that." His eyes scanned the pass for any sign of his horse. "Have you seen my horse?"

"I haven't, but Gray Fox has. He tried to bring her down to you, but your dog wouldn't let him near the horse."

"Shep is a good dog." His head pounded. "What happened to me?"

Matt giggled. "Promise you won't try to kill me?"

"Why would I do that?"

"Because I hit you on the head with a stone."

"Why did you hit me?"

"Because you were going to hurt my friend."

"I was concerned as to what he was going to do to you."

She sat back and wiggled her toes. "We were playing."

Cute little toes were attached to small narrow feet and he admired them. "That's not the way a gentleman plays with a young woman."

Her wiggling stopped and she bolted upright, fisting her hands. "I'm no girl."

"Mattie, don't hit me." The throbbing in his head wasn't going away. "Once was enough. I'm probably going to die from this pain, anyway."

"Don't call me Mattie. I'm not a girl."

"No, you're not a girl. You're a woman. Don't ask me how I know, because I don't want to lie."

"What makes you think I'm a woman?"

"Don't ask me that. I know you are, so stop denying it. All I want to know is why the pretense?"

Matilda laid back and stared at the cloudless sky for a moment. Gray Fox knew she was a girl and he didn't care. She looked at the stranger beside her. "Who are you?"

He stuck out his hand at her and said, "Zeke Hillerman. I work for the Haas stockyard on the other side of Hanover. Mr. Van Dyke orders cattle about once a month and I drive them here."

"I'm Matilda Berwyn." She sat up and took his hand. "My pa hides the fact that I'm a girl. He says it's safer for me with all the men around here."

"And you think it's safe to wander off alone and keep a Lakota as a friend?"

"Gray Fox is my friend. And no one bothers me out here. No one even knows I'm here."

"I knew you came here."

She scrunched up her nose. "You do? Um, you did?"

"And you are panning for gold. What do you expect to find in this stream?"

A feeling of panic ran up her back. *I can't let anyone know about my box.* "I like to pretend I'm finding tons of gold, and that I can run away and have my very own house filled with books, and that I can wear pretty dresses, and—"

"Whoa." He held up his hand. "Pretending isn't going to make anything happen. You need to make serious plans."

"I am making plans."

"Doesn't sound like it and a woman just can't run off alone."

"Why not?"

"Because proper ladies don't do things like that."

"But once I have money, I can do anything, right?"

He grimaced and put his hand to his head.

Uncertain if his frown was over what she had said or if his head hurt, she reached into her pocket for the bark Gray Fox had given her. "Here. This might help your head."

He took the strip of bark but fished next to where she was sitting. "You are panning for gold. Just how many of these have you found?"

The little nugget must have rolled from her pocket. "Give it back!"

He bounced it in his hand before dropping the marble-sized ball into her outstretched hand. "I'm not taking it from you, but that must be worth a whole bunch of dresses. I'd say it was a couple of ounces."

Panic was now mixing with curiosity. "What do you know about gold?"

"Almost nothing, but I know how much a handful of nails weigh." He held out the piece of bark. "What's this, willow?"

She nodded. "Don't tell anyone. I didn't steal the gold. I found it."

"In this creek?"

She nodded again. "Don't tell anyone about me."

He stuck the piece of willow in his mouth and sucked on it. "Your secrets are safe with me."

"If you tell anyone, I'll kill you and I mean it."

"You probably would kill me."

Matilda and Zeke chatted until she said she had to leave. Her father and brother would be expecting their dinner and she hadn't even started to make anything. He watched her scamper away. There was nothing boyish about her. The clothes that she wore and the cut of her hair said male, but everything else screamed female. He hauled himself to his feet and slowly made his way to his horse.

He ate some food, ate, and shared some with Shep. With luck, he'd be home by late morning. The land was parched. What should have been green wasn't. But contemplating the weather was beyond him. He needed to stay awake long enough to return to the stockyard.

Three times, he caught himself asleep in the saddle. Each time, he wondered how he'd managed to drift off with his pounding headache. The willow bark didn't seem to help, and he didn't want to poison himself. He fought to keep his eyes open, but they seemed to fail at staying focused. *The stockyard. I have to get to the stockyard.*

TWO

Zeke awakened to his own room. "What?"

"Don't move," the Haas's foreman, Clay, said. "I'll find Cook. She's been mighty worried about you."

A few moments later, Cook burst into the room with the biggest smile. "Thought we were going to lose you, young man. That was quite a fever you stirred up. And whatever happened to you?"

He reached into the back of his mind and tried to recall what happened to him on the ride home. "I can't remember much other than trying to stay awake. How did I get here?"

Clay answered, "Shep came first, barking his head off, and then I saw you all slumped over and half out of the saddle. I brought you into the kitchen and let my wife take care of you."

"Oh, what a sight you were! A bloody bandage all stuck to your head. Terrible, terrible. We've been waiting for days for you to wake up. But you are back with us now, and I'll bring you some food."

He lost track of time as he ate and slept, but each time he opened his eyes, there was something delicious waiting for him. Morning noises awakened him and he discovered he could raise his head without feeling as though it would explode. Slowly he stood and realized he wasn't dizzy. The fever that had wracked his system had abated, and he felt normal, yet still weak. He made his way to the privy behind the barn, and then washed up at the sink in the barn. In the small mirror over the sink, he could see that there had to have been at least a week's worth of whiskers on his face. He found his razor and pulled it over the strop a few times before attempting to lather his face and remove the beard.

As he rinsed his face, Cook entered the barn. Her curls were longer than Mattie's and more red than orange.

"There you are and looking like a new man. How are you feeling?"

"Starved."

"Then I think you will be pleased with breakfast. We've been lucky to make you eat three bites of anything." She put the tray of food on the small table they all shared in the living quarters of the barn. "Have a seat while I inspect that wound on your head."

His body tensed as she ran her fingers through his hair, but this time there was no pain, only a slight dull ache as she pressed around the gash. "How bad is it?"

"It's closed now."

"Mattie did that."

"Did what?"

"Put the stitch in my head." He scooped up a forkful of eggs.

"Who is Mattie?"

"A girl. Seemed to know what she was doing."

Cook harrumphed. "She should have cleaned that wound before stitching it closed. Had to open it, clean it, and put a new stitch in it. How did you manage such a cut in the first place? Fall off your horse?"

"It's complicated. I was trying to help her and that's the last I remember. Woke up with her at my side and the most wicked headache imaginable."

Cook shook her head. "Clay says you aren't allowed to do anything for a few days. I suspect that Mr. Haas will be out to see you. We've all been worried about you."

Zeke nodded as he ate his breakfast. Then he washed it down with a cup of coffee. He wasn't certain that he wanted to talk with Mr. Haas, not yet. Not until he sorted out what all had happened.

Matilda discovered that even her routine chores didn't feel the same. Zeke stayed on her mind. Unsure of his age, she only knew he was older. His handsome face with pretty blue eyes, and his blond hair that was neatly trimmed seemed to appear in her mind at the oddest of times. She wanted to look pretty for him and tried extra hard to comb her hair into some sort of style, but it fell in ringlets and refused to be tamed. *About once a month.* She began to count the number of days until she thought she might see him again.

Her little golden spot had yielded two more boxes of nuggets and then it seemed to come to an end. She moved upstream and found nothing. She moved downstream and found nothing. Her dreams of finding more gold were coming to an end.

One morning as she ran errands for the company store, she had to go to Mr. Van Dyke's house and he showed her inside.

"I brought you the items from the store."

"Thank you, Matt. Take them straight back and leave them on the table."

"I will, sir. Excuse me, may I ask you a question?"

"Certainly. But don't expect me to have all the answers."

She wrinkled her nose. "Who actually buys gold?"

"Ultimately, the U.S. Treasury."

"So you take it to someone?"

He nodded.

"What would someone do if they only had a little bit of gold?"

He raised his eyebrows.

"I mean if someone found a piece of gold."

"How big and where?"

She curled her thumb and forefinger into a tight circle. "It's the size of a pea and it's mine. I found it fair and square in a creek. It caught my eye in the sunlight."

"Did you look for more?"

She nodded.

"Follow me."

He took her to a room with a desk and pulled a map out of a drawer. "Show me where you found it."

She put the package she was carrying on the table next to the map. "This is where I live and…" She traced her finger along the creek to where it crossed the red lines that had been drawn around the mountain. "I'm thinking it would be about here."

He stared hard at her. "If you are telling the truth, young man, it's yours fair and square." He raised his eyebrows. "Are you sure you didn't find any more? How hard did you search?"

She smiled at him. "I'm not stupid. I looked hard for anything I could find."

He traced his finger around an area on the map "If it was found within these lines, it would have been my gold according to my registration. If you've found more, then you would be entitled to stake your own claim." His finger settled on the spot she had showed him. "I'd help you fill out those papers."

"No, sir. I promise, I looked really hard."

"If you'd like to bring it to me, I'll pay you for it."

"I'd like to keep it, at least for now. But please don't tell Pa. If he knows about it, he'll want it, and it's mine."

"It's a deal." Mr. Van Dyke held out his hand and Matilda took it.

"Thanks, Mr. Van Dyke. It was found and not stolen. And it wasn't on your property."

"I believe you, Matt." He ruffled Matilda's hair. "It's not

unusual to find small amounts of gold in the streams out here. Many a man has staked a claim to a spot and totally missed the mother load. Chances are hundreds of years ago that piece you found was part of a mountain, but winds and rain over time washed it to where you found it."

"If I had been really lucky, I would have found more?"

He nodded. "You're a good boy, and when you're running errands, you're often handling goods worth more than that little nugget of gold."

"Thank you, sir. I'd never steal. That's one of the Ten Commandments. There's nothing here on earth worth my going to Hell."

Mr. Van Dyke chuckled and picked up her package. "Go run the rest of your errands. I know Roscoe Jones has plenty of them this morning, being it is payday."

She nodded and scurried from the house. The gold really was hers fair and square, but she'd have to get to a big town to sell it. *A pretty dress in green and some fancy earrings to go with it.*

Half way between Mr. Van Dyke's house and the store, another thought struck. *Payday. One month! Zeke should be coming tomorrow!*

Zeke looked at the odd load he was taking. He had twenty-five chickens loaded in cages in a buckboard along with two penned pigs. He was supposed to drive the cart plus three heads of cattle and two lambs. "Shep, we have our work cut out for us this time."

Clay laughed. "Talking to the dog as if he were human?"

"He has to work like one on this trip." A chuckle rolled up the back of Zeke's throat. "He's probably better than most cowboys when it comes to driving."

"At least he doesn't complain." Clay jerked his thumb over his shoulder in the direction of the dog. "The way his tail is wagging, I reckon he's looking forward to it." He crossed his arms over his chest. "Heard that Van Dyke has quite an operation going there. I can understand wanting some food supplies handy."

"These sheep aren't for butchering. Seems one of the ladies there wants some high quality wool."

Clay ran his hand over the back of the one lamb. "It's a mystery how this becomes yarn." Clay chortled. "Growing socks for miners, old girl? I've heard the way to Hell is through the icy cold belly of a mountain. It starts out cold, and the closer you go to Hell, the hotter the mountain is."

Clay's comment took Zeke by surprise. "Why would you say that?"

"Dangerous work and they all know it. They work hard and they drink hard. It's not a good life." Clay continued to pet the lamb and she bleated her approval. "What we do isn't easy, but it's a better way of life. When was the last time you were hungry?"

Zeke shook his head. "I've missed a meal or two in my life, but I've never thought I was going to starve to death."

"Won't happen if you have dirt and water. You rely on

someone other than yourself, and you are in trouble."

"It's not like this is your land."

Clay motioned towards the house. "That man is relying on the railroad, and other ranchers. My job is taking care of this land and the animals on it."

Zeke nodded. "Good point. I want my own piece of land. I thought I was running away from the farm, instead I've discovered I'm going back to the land."

Tipping his hat at Clay and climbing onto the buckboard's seat, Zeke knew he was ready. He'd never make it through the passes with a cart so he was forced to travel the southern route.

The man has his opinion and I have mine. I can farm a few acres and put the rest into grazing. Those thoughts rumbled through Zeke's mind as he formulated his plan to have a ranch. He'd seen hard times. There were too many cattle on too few acres, and everyone expected the grass to be there.

Zeke thought back to the lessons his father had taught him. *Multiple crops - never rely on a single crop and plant plenty of vegetables.* He could almost hear his father's voice as he slapped the reins.

Zeke listened to some squawks, bleats, and a grumbling moo as he started on his way. He had ample responsibility on this trip but that didn't worry him. He only wanted to see Mattie.

Matilda sat on the wide wooden boards of the store's porch. The town consisted of several wooden buildings and a few houses, most in varying shades of aging, cut timber. She wondered when people would decide to paint. Her thoughts went to the home she'd once known in California. Instead of sod, it was made of mud. But the houses and buildings were often painted in various bright colors. Watching the traffic while she sucked on her sassafras-flavored candy stick was something to do. Not that there was much traffic on the dirt road that ran through the mining town. The miners were either home asleep or at the mine, leaving a few women to meet, shop, and gossip. She didn't care about their gossip. Chances were she probably already knew it.

Everyone treated her like a halfwit child and assumed she wouldn't know if a rattlesnake bit her. But she knew what she saw. She knew Calvin would sneak over to Miz Mable's house after her husband went to the mine. And she knew Henry was doing more than drinking beer at the saloon even though he had a wife. Except Matilda had no clue why anyone would want to talk about it. But she did like to see the ladies with their pretty dresses, not that many wore them, only a few, and the rest wore plain or calico cotton without bustles or fancy lace. A friend of Miz Rosalind's walked past wearing a pretty blue dress trimmed in white and she had fancy ear bobs that matched her dress.

Matilda wondered how the women managed to keep those dresses clean. She almost never saw one hanging on a clothesline, at least not a pretty dress such as the ones these fancy ladies wore. Many times she'd seen what they wore under those dresses, for she had seen those items hanging on lines to dry. Matilda promised herself that she would wear a corset even though it looked like something impossible to wear with all those laces that had to be tied. *Oh, yes! I will be a proper lady.*

When her candy stick was done she wandered towards the tents. At the edge of the tent area there was a well pump. She raised the handle and as she lowered it, water burst from the pump. She rinsed her hands in the well water and then splashed some on her face. Cupping her hand, she slurped some water and rinsed her mouth. Between the grit from the mine and the dirt road, the cold water not only washed the grime and the sticky sweetness away, it felt good after being in the hot sun.

She walked down the road towards the stream. There was a bridge there and on the other side was the Talbot ranch. It wasn't much of a bridge, just a few planks, but it felt like the world existed on the other side. She stood on the bridge and looked at the stream. A twig snapped behind her and she turned in the direction of the sound but saw nothing.

To say she was bored was an understatement. She wanted a book to read, something to whisk her away from her life in Homestead Canyon. Her mind went to her golden spot. Whatever was there, she had collected. Now there was nothing. *How far do I dare go from Homestead Canyon to find more?* Gray Fox said he had looked in the stream, too, and he never found any more gold. Even his people wanted it. Her mind tried to calculate the amount of gold she had found, but she came up blank. She had no clue as to how pure it was or what it was worth.

Her imagination came up just as blank when she wondered what it would be like to live in a grand house. *How long would it take me to walk to Hanover?* Another sound caused her to look around, and again, she saw nothing. *Maybe I'm imagining it.*

The following morning she couldn't wait to get away from the soddy. Certain that Zeke was coming, she gathered the family laundry and ran along the stream until she reached a spot where she could see Zeke as he came through the pass. She waded into the knee-high water and washed the clothes, but her gaze constantly swept the path through the mountains.

A sound jerked her attention to a spot behind her. After studying the area carefully, she decided there was nothing there. She went back to washing. Hearing another sound, she turned. This time she saw something. It might have been a prairie dog or maybe a rat. She wasn't certain, because it vanished into some undergrowth. *I must stop this. I can't be looking over my shoulder every three seconds. What is wrong with me?*

But she couldn't shake the feeling that she was being watched. Her skin prickled and she was covered in gooseflesh even though the sun beating on her back was hot. She washed her arms and face. Then made the decision to stick her head into the water and wash her hair. She held her eyes tightly closed, for if the soapsuds went into her eyes, it would sting like bees. But the sound of twigs snapping sent her heart racing. She rinsed quickly, opened her eyes, and scanned the area. Soap-laced water droplets found their way to her eyes. Dunking her head one more time, she rubbed her burning eyes. When she opened her eyes, she was certain she saw someone.

Normally she would have placed the wet clothes on some bushes to dry, but today she didn't want to wait. She gathered up her things and started walking down the stream. She'd been walking this stream for years and knew its hazards. If someone wanted her, they'd have to come into the stream and she was certain she had the advantage.

The entire way back to the soddy, she kept her knife tightly clutched in her hand and hidden under the clothes. But when she reached the soddy, she realized she was still in danger. Her father had tucked it in a copse of trees and then planted what he called rushin' bushes. They were pretty and dense, but they had large thorns. The birds loved them for nesting and they had created a barrier around the house, but also trapped her. As fast as she could, she spread the clothes over those bushes and sprinted into town.

Her pants were soaked well above her knees and her shirt was wet from her hair dripping water off her curls and the rest of her shirt was wet from carrying wet clothes. She looked at herself with total disgust. *I look as though I've been swimming with my clothes on.* The sun shone on the boardinghouse steps, so she sat there and slumped, hoping she'd dry quickly and not call attention to herself.

Reviewing everything she had done and what she had seen didn't shake the uneasiness that stayed with her. She wished Gray Fox hadn't gone to the prairie to hunt with his family. The need for an extra person to watch to see who was following her... *If I could make myself a twin...* Silently, she chuckled.

Lena walked down the street. Her pretty white dress was printed in flowers and bits of lace peeked out from the hem, sleeves, and bodice. Her blonde hair was pulled up and Matilda couldn't wait to see what Lena had done to her hair this time. Seems it was always tied in some sort of matching ribbon. *Oh, I want dresses like Lena's, all pretty and feminine.*

Matilda raised her hand in a wave. She was certain that they were close in age. Lena smiled back and lifted her delicate hand in acknowledgement. *Wonder what you'd do if you knew I was a woman?*

Lena went into the store and that's when Matilda could see that Lena had wrapped her hair into a tight knot at the nape of her neck and tied it with some pink ribbon that matched the flowers in her dress. Lena's skin was fair and she looked so beautiful. Matilda looked at her arms covered in more freckles than there were stars in the sky. Freckles butted against freckles giving her arms a reddish brown look and the freckles continued to the edges of her fingernails.

The noon whistle blew at the mine. Four times a day it blew; at noon, midnight, five o'clock in the morning and five o'clock in the evening. She figured it was more for the residents then the miners because once inside the belly of the mountain, the miners couldn't hear a whistle. Sometimes she hated the sound, and at others, those whistles often meant she had enough time to hurry home before her father arrived.

Heat had probably kept most residents inside and out of the noonday sun. The town was quiet, only the sound of the stamp could be heard. That thing never stopped. Its job was to crush the stone so that the copper could be separated from it. She barely heard the pounding noise, for she had grown accustomed to the sound from the time she was small. In fact, when it quit was when she noticed the quiet, but that meant trouble if the stamp stopped for more than a few minutes. And trouble meant her father would come home grumpy and take out his frustration on her. *I hate that!*

Someplace in the distance she heard mooing. It took a moment for the sound to register and then she jumped from where she sat. Shielding her eyes from the sun, she looked towards the paddock. There was activity there and she wasn't certain why. Zeke hadn't come. Then another thought crossed her mind. *What if Mr. Van Dyke bought his cattle elsewhere and Zeke will never come again?*

Her guts tightened. There was something about Zeke she liked. She wanted him to return, wanted to smile, and flirt with him. His smile twinkled in his eyes even when he was hurt. *What if he doesn't want to see me?*

That day flashed through her mind. The memory of the terrible gash on his head lingered. *He doesn't want to see me.* She scuffed one foot through the dirt and watched as puffs of pale dirt rose a few inches and then settled down, dusting her feet in the fine grit. *No male wants me.*

Then she saw Shep. "Shep!" She took off in a run. "Shep. Shep!"

The dog turned and snarled at her.

She heard Zeke say, "Easy, boy. What's your problem?"

"Zeke!"

He turned and smiled. "Hello, Matt. Come to help me?"

She could feel her smile. "Certainly."

Bone-aching tiredness kept him moving, but all he wanted was some food and sleep. This trip had been slower. He figured he'd been awake for over thirty-six hours. "Push those chicken crates to the end and I'll take them off the back.

Matilda nodded and climbed up as if it were nothing. He remembered his sisters who would have balked at being asked to do such a thing in their skirts. But Mattie did it as though it was a simple request.

"You've met Matt?" Mr. Van Dyke raised his eyebrows.

Zeke nodded as he lifted the one crate and set it on the ground. "We met the last time I came here." He swept his gaze to Mattie and caught her frown. "He's tough for his size."

"His dad and brother are fair-sized men. I figure Matt is a late bloomer. One of these days, he'll shoot up tall like his older brother. Until then, he keeps his dad and brother fed." Mr. Van Dyke checked each cage.

"They are all healthy, Mr. Van Dyke. Mr. Haas wouldn't send anything that wasn't."

"Never had a problem with anything from his stockyard. He has quality animals at fair prices."

Zeke looked at the man who was probably in his thirties. "I've learned a lot working for him. I grew up on a farm, but once our animals were sold, I had no clue what happened to them. It's been a good experience."

Mr. Van Dyke clapped his hand on Zeke's back. "You're a smart young man. Learn as much as you can in your chosen field."

"Thank you, sir. That's all of them, sir. I hope you are satisfied." Zeke fished in his pocket for some change.

"I certainly am and I'm positive you're looking for a place to sleep." He motioned to a spot behind him. "Pull your cart into the shade."

Mattie spoke up. "If you ride down there by the stream, your mules can enjoy the water."

"That sounds good to me. Any chance you can find someone to sell me a few fresh and hearty sandwiches?" He dropped several coins in Matilda's palm. "I'm sick of jerky. And Shep could use some food, too."

"The boardinghouse. Follow me."

He bid Mr. Van Dyke a good day and followed Mattie down the road.

"There's a well pump there with good water. Fill your canteen and then head over there while I buy your sandwiches."

"Make that one sandwich for me and one for you. Is there a bakery around here?"

She shook her head. "I'll do my best."

He did as he was told and found a spot by the stream. It was slightly secluded and he liked that. He wanted to talk to Mattie without being overheard. Actually, he wanted to do more than talk, but his parents had raised him to be a gentleman.

By the time he had managed to secure the mules, Mattie

returned with a basket of food.

"That was quick."

Mattie smiled. "Miz Beatrice was in the kitchen. Didn't take her but a few minutes."

Zeke took the basket and peered inside expecting something less than wonderful. Instead, he found two beautiful, golden-brown rolls with a heavy slice of meatloaf tucked into each one, several carrots, and what appeared to be oatmeal cookies, all tucked next to a big jar of sweet milk and another of something dark. He lifted the dark jar and stared at it.

"Coffee."

He nodded and handed the glass jar of milk to Mattie. "Ladies are served first."

Mattie cocked her head.

He grinned and handed her a striped napkin and a sandwich. "I just hope I can stay awake long enough to eat."

"I'm sorry you're that tired. I'll sneak some supper out to you after my father goes to bed."

"I'd appreciate it."

As much as he wanted to visit with Mattie, he couldn't stay awake another minute. With his bedroll on a soft pile of leaves and his tummy filled, he closed his eyes. He opened them when she brought him some potato and ham soup. Then he closed his eyes again. He woke up once and realized he had two hard-boiled eggs, but drifted off again.

Morning sunlight filtered between the leaves overhead. He opened his eyes and stretched. Every part of him felt renewed and ready for the day. Standing, he swung his arms in a crossed pattern in front of him and then swung them as far back as he could. After doing that several times, he knew he had recuperated. He sat, ate the two eggs, and drank the coffee that he had found waiting for him. He knew he'd slept for almost twenty-four hours.

Hearing noise on the far side of the stream put him on alert. Then he saw a man walking towards the mining town. He was short and wiry with a generous mustache. The man acted as though he didn't notice anyone around him.

A few minutes later, Mattie came downstream, looking as though she'd taken a bath.

Zeke chuckled as he approached Mattie. "Hello. Bathing?"

She nodded and ran her fingers through her wet curls.

He couldn't help the smirk that he was certain showed on his face. "I would have enjoyed watching you."

Her fist connected with his upper arm.

"Ow! That really hurt."

"You're not very polite. Men aren't supposed to be watching."

"Well, the first time I didn't know you. Now that I do…"

"What?" Her eyes were almost squeezed shut with her displeasure.

"Give me your hands."

"Why?"

"Dammit. I want to show you something." His insides throbbed as his heart beat faster.

She put her hands out to him and he captured her wrists.

"Because a beautiful woman makes a man's heart race." He

put her hands to his chest. "And your copper-colored curls and sun-kissed body… I've never had a woman that made me feel the way you do."

She gazed up at him. Her green eyes were filled with flecks of gold, brown, and blue.

His heart beat faster and his desire for her burned like coal. "Let me show you what you do to me."

He pulled her closer to him and pressed his lips to hers.

She didn't exactly kiss him back.

He moved away from her mouth and let his lips trail across her cheek to her ear. He nibbled on her lobe and then drifted down her neck. He heard her whimper, as she pressed her body to his. "Oh, Mattie. I can't wait to see you dressed, as you deserve to be. You will turn the head of every man for miles. Just remember you are mine."

She whimpered again like a new kitten. He kissed her one more time on the lips. This time she responded and he thought his insides were going to explode. She pressed her palms flat to his chest and pushed away. He knew to let her go.

He exhaled and watched her do the same. "Mattie, you are beautiful. Since that first time I saw you, there's not a night I've fallen asleep without thinking of you… without wondering what it would be like to hold you in my arms and kiss you."

"I need to go."

"No, you don't, Mattie. You're just scared, afraid of your feelings, and concerned I will do more. I won't. I'm a good man, Mattie. With luck in a few months, I'll have my own ranch. I've been saving for it."

"You're leaving?"

Mattie's heart broke into two pieces. She took off as fast as her feet could carry her. He was on her heels, but she wasn't going to let up. Her lungs burned, but he stayed with her the entire time. Darting into the meadow, she threw her body into the dry grass. She didn't care what happened to her. The thought of Zeke leaving her was more than she could handle.

She felt Zeke's body against hers and his arm wrapping around her. His breath was ragged and she realized she was feeling his chest as it rose and fell. The feeling of being paralyzed gripped her, yet she knew she needed to get up and continue running until he could no longer chase her.

"Mattie, talk to me. Why are you running?" He heaved the words between deep breaths.

What is there to say? I don't want you to leave. Don't take my hopes away from me? "Take me with you," she mumbled.

He rolled her onto her back.

She covered her eyes to protect them from the blaring sun. "Don't leave me. I hate it here."

"I'm not going for a few months. And I can't exactly just snatch you. It wouldn't be proper. We're not married. Besides, don't you think we need time to know each other?"

"I don't have secrets." *Well maybe I do.* "What do you want to know?"

"What are we supposed to know about another person?"

"I'm tired of hiding the fact that I'm a female. I hate living in the soddy. I want a real house like Mr. Van Dyke's, and I want to go to school."

Zeke rolled over on his back and let out a sigh. "There are colleges in Pennsylvania for women, but you can't go there if you are married and they are expensive. I'm certain there are other colleges for women that aren't as far away but... I think you must have a high school diploma"

"If I don't go to school, then I want books - lots of books." She sat up and looked at him. His blond hair was mussed and tiny wisps were plastered to his perspiration-soaked forehead.

"Mattie, I don't know what to tell you. You must decide. I want a ranch, and I'm going to have one."

"Don't leave me here." She plucked some grass from his hair, and then rested her hand on his shirt-covered chest. Blond chest hair poked over his partially open shirt. The desire to touch and see him almost overwhelmed her.

"I'll take you with me, when I leave the stockyard." He raised his hand to shield his face from the sun. "I save almost everything I make. I want that ranch and from what I've heard, there's good land here in Wyoming. But I doubt it will be easy in the beginning. You can't transform raw land into a ranch overnight nor can I build a house in three days. It all takes time."

"Can't be worse than living here."

"Don't count on it. Until I can build a barn and a house, we might be living in a tent."

That's not what she wanted to hear. "I want a grand house and pretty dresses."

"Mattie, be reasonable. It won't happen overnight."

She ran her fingertips over the soft hair on his arms. Part of her didn't care if she had to live in an open field. She leaned down and this time she kissed him.

He wrapped his arms around her and pressed his lips tightly to hers. He rolled her onto her back and covered her body with his. Her arms circled his neck and she could hear herself mewing.

She didn't want him to stop or for the delicious, tingly feeling to go away.

Zeke let go of Mattie. He knew what they were doing was wrong. He looked at her swollen and bruised lips. *What have I done?* "Mattie, we can't do this. It's wrong."

"But if feels wonderful."

He nodded, knowing he had no words to explain it. Looking one more time into her colorful green eyes, he forced himself to his feet and then gave his hand to her, pulling her to her feet. "We must not do that again."

Guilt stabbed him in the abdomen.

She removed the dried grass that clung to him. "We both can't look as though we've been rolling in the grass. No one will pay any attention to a young boy covered in debris."

He shook his head. "Maybe being a boy is a good thing. No one will suspect anything." He smiled at her. "You do read and write, don't you?"

"Of course!"

"Then we can write to each other when I'm not here."

"I have no paper or pens."

His smile widened. "Then I will make certain you do."

They walked back into town and he went to his spot near the livery. He needed to prepare to leave for the stockyard. But his plans were interrupted with a crack of thunder and the splatter of raindrops. He ran to the livery and its protective covering. After watching the water stream off the roof for what seemed like an hour, he gave up and found a spot to nap. He awakened once with the late afternoon whistle, and again, with the midnight whistle. Each time, the rain hitting the tin roof of the livery was almost deafening. He was forced to wait until it stopped. But before the morning whistle at the mine blew, the rain had come to an end.

He stepped out of the livery and into the fresh air. Inhaling deeply, the scent of rain still lingered and mixed with the scent of trees, animals, and grasses, making everything smell clean and fresh. Small channels had been made where the rain had hit the dirt-covered road and ran. The storm had been too hard, too much, and too fast. It didn't soak the ground.

He found a privy and used it. Then he washed his face at the pump by the metal shop. The mules looked content and the buckboard was washed clean. He gazed up at the sky and offered his thanks, for that had saved him from a smelly job of cleaning chicken droppings and pig manure from the boards. The morning whistle blew.

The sun hadn't risen into sight, but the sky no longer twinkled in stars. John Thorpe came across the road and handed him two thick slabs of toasted bread spread with lemon cream. "I thought you might be hungry and the saloon isn't open at this hour."

"Thank you, sir. This is much appreciated."

It was delicious. He ate every bite and licked his fingers. "Hope no one minded me sleeping in here last night."

"Not a problem. I saw you make the dash for it. That storm was wicked, but we needed the rain. I was worried we'd have another summer like last year."

"Don't need one of those."

"Certainly don't." The man raised his hand in a wave. "I've work to do."

Zeke held up his hand. "Thanks for the breakfast, sir."

He called to his mules and began to hitch them to the cart. He turned from what he was doing to find a small woman standing behind him.

"Mrs. Van Dyke said to bring this to you." The woman's accent was strong.

"Thank you, ma'am. Please tell Mrs. Van Dyke that it's much appreciated." White paper was wrapped around a beautiful roll that had been split open and slathered in butter. Next to it was a slab of fried meat and two hard-boiled eggs that had been peeled. He shared part of the meat and an egg with Shep before devouring the rest of it.

Totally full, he prepared to leave. He could see the men walking to the mine and noticed several redheads. One was an older man with a younger man beside him. The younger one looked very much like Mattie. *That must be her father and brother.* He tried not to stare, but he wanted to know who these people were. Both men carried buckets, and Zeke knew the buckets were filled with food. Mattie would feed them before she would eat. He shook his head and wondered how anyone could be so cruel to a child. *My children will never suffer. Never!*

As he rode towards town, he spotted Mattie and went to her.

"I brought you some breakfast. I don't want you leaving here with an empty belly." She handed him two slabs of what looked like cornbread with bits of fruit and nuts in it, and between the layers was an egg that had been creamed. The combination seemed a bit unusual, but her smile was so contagious that he willingly took a bite of her offering. Then wished he hadn't. He swallowed. "Did you eat?"

She nodded.

"Mind if I save this? Seems you are the third person to hand me food this morning."

"Go right ahead. I was worried because the saloon isn't open, and the boardinghouse might not have anything. Who fed you?"

"John Thorpe and Mrs. Van Dyke."

"I've heard that Mrs. Van Dyke makes the most perfect rolls. I wish she would teach me, but it's rare that I ever have any white flour." She scrunched up her nose.

"Those days will end. Flour is cheap."

"No it's not. There's barely enough money to feed us. That's why I'm always searching for whatever I can find in the way of berries and nuts."

"I will send you pens, paper, and envelopes. What else do you need?"

"Everything and nothing." Then she beamed him a big smile.

"Nothing is easy and everything will take me a little while." He looked around him. "Wait for me, Mattie. Remember you are mine. But I must leave here."

She nodded and waved to him. "Goodbye."

"Write to me."

"I will, I promise."

He slapped the reins. Part of him was shattering, as he wanted to take her to the stockyard with him. He knew he should have never kissed her the way he had. They were not sweet chaste kisses that a man was supposed to give a young woman he was courting. Instead, they were hungry and passionate.

THREE

The mercantile in Hanover was not exactly what he was expecting. Many times he'd gone with his mother and sisters to Germantown for supplies. The stores there were lovely and filled with wonderful items, but this store was filled with bits of everything and seemed crammed with things. He walked around for a few minutes until a man came and asked if he could help.

"I need a pen, ink, paper, envelopes…"

The man showed Zeke several fancy sets.

"No, sir, something plain. Um, something a young boy might use?"

The man dug through a pile of stuff and produced the perfect thing. The small wooden box held everything and the paper inside was plain.

"And do you have any books?"

The man pointed to another spot in the store.

Zeke checked the stacks of books and found several by Mark Twain and then another book on American history. "These three. Will you put them with the paper set and mail them?"

It was more money than he wanted to spend, but he had never lacked for anything while he was growing up, and even now, he had everything he needed. Anything else was extra. But he would have done this for Matt, even if he were a boy.

Working for Mr. Haas wasn't easy. The hours were often long and the actual work was physically difficult, but at the end of the day, Zeke would sit on the Haas' back porch and eat a hearty meal that would rival anything his mom made.

Often Mr. Haas would join Zeke and discuss the day. He looked forward to the man's visits and listened attentively as he explained everything. From what Mr. Haas said, his life wasn't much different. He had worked and learned as he went. Each job he held added to his knowledge and each had provided valuable information. He willingly passed that information along to Zeke, knowing that one day, in the near future, Zeke would leave to start is own ranch. Mr. Haas seemed to like protégés succeeding. If Zeke had a profitable ranch that meant more income for the stockyard.

Other times, the two little Haas girls, Phyllis and Suzanne would come out and play. They'd often beg for someone to saddle their pony and he couldn't resist their little angelic faces. Phyllis reminded him so much of his one sister in looks, but his sister was more like Suzanne in personality. No matter how tired he was he'd saddle the pony and walk with the girls.

But every night in the waning evening light, he'd write to Mattie. Their letters were delayed by several days because the mail didn't go to Homestead Canyon every day. When her first letter arrived, he was called to the house to retrieve it. He almost leapt for joy. He tucked it in his shirt and waited until he was completely alone to read it.

Guilt still clung to him. He couldn't shake the feeling. He had kissed other young women, but he'd never kissed anyone the way he had kissed Mattie. No matter how he tried to dislodge the feeling or excuse his behavior, he couldn't. What he had done was wrong.

It was after the sun had vanished from the sky that Zeke had a chance to read the letter. He sat on the fence behind the barn and pulled the letter from his shirt pocket. Her letter was full of hope and dreams, but also of fear.

If you think someone is following you, someone probably is. He thought about the time before he knew her when he watched her bathe. If he discovered her, it was easy to believe that someone else had. And that could put her in great danger. He immediately wrote and told her to be extremely careful. *'You need to find a better place. Maybe someplace closer to town, where if you needed, you could call for help.'*

Leaving her there wasn't safe. He needed take her far away from Homestead Canyon. If another man had discovered her secret, then it was possible that man may have shared that knowledge.

Putting her on a train to his parents was one possibility, but it wasn't respectable or prudent for a young woman to travel alone. He couldn't bring her to the stockyard, and he didn't know Hanover well enough to know if there was someplace where she could stay. But as he mulled over the situation, he realized if she traveled as a young man. Time… He needed time to sort this out and to tell his parents.

When Matilda received Zeke's letter, she could tell that she had upset him. *Nothing will happen to me. I can take care of myself.* But the idea of going far away to a big city like Philadelphia appealed to her. Certainly they would be able to trade her gold for cash.

She ran errands that morning for Mr. Van Dyke and for Miz Rosalind, but instead of taking penny candy, she asked if they would run a tab for her, she wanted something bigger.

Miz Rosalind grinned. "It's going to take more than a handful of pennies for a dictionary, Matt."

"Oh, I know that. I need a new toothbrush and a can of tooth powder." She looked at the toothbrushes on the display board and knew she wanted the nice one. She'd have to run several sets of errands before she could afford to buy a bone-handled toothbrush with boar bristles.

Miz Rosalind nodded. "We can run a tab for you, but why don't you put it on your father's account?"

Matilda squared her shoulders. "Because I'm not a little boy anymore, and I want to be responsible for my own things."

"Very admirable. I'll set up an account in your name."

Pleased, Matilda stepped out of the company store and headed back to the soddy. When she approached the place she referred to as home, her skin began to crawl. The feeling of being watched was too much. She turned around and went back towards town. Zigzagging between some tents, she watched to see who might be strolling around. It seemed like forever, but no one stirred.

She gave up and returned to town. Ruby and Jolene from the saloon walked to the store and then Miz Beatrice. In the distance, Matilda saw Yanyu. The way she moved with tiny steps, she always appeared to be in a big hurry. Matilda had seen plenty of Chinese women when she was in California, but Yanyu seemed different and Matilda didn't know why.

There wasn't a single person in Homestead Canyon that she didn't know, and everyone was friendly towards her. *So who would be following me, and why?*

Her mind wandered to Ruby and Jolene. Matilda had been warned by her father to stay away from the gals at the saloon, but they were both nice women. Then Lena caught her eye. Dressed in white with pink trim, and a fancy crocheted shawl, Matilda decided that of all the women in Homestead Canyon, she loved Lena's clothes best of all. Lena didn't walk to town this time. She walked to the livery where her husband worked. *Taking him dinner?*

Aside from a few women, there wasn't a single man to be found stirring in town. Giving up, Matilda went home, but as she approached the soddy, she had that same feeling of being watched. Gooseflesh raised on her arms and the nape of her neck prickled. Instead of going into the soddy, she walked around the back of it.

This morning she had fixed hot oat cereal for her brother and father. Oats always took forever to cook. She boiled the water and then added the oats. The minute she did, she saw a problem – weevils. She had added extra water when she realized the number of weevils that were in the oats, and then carefully spooned out the weevils that floated to the top as the cereal boiled. Certain she'd removed most of them, she added a bit of fatback to give the oats more flavor and let it boil down. Now she had a messy pan. Lifting the pan from the stove, she looked at the oat cereal that was stuck to the metal, and headed for the stream.

Instead of staying in a secluded area, she walked to the plank bridge near the tents and placed the pan into the cool water. It wasn't much of a pan, but if she left it, someone would probably take it. She yanked her pants above her knees and waded into the water. She rubbed her arms and face with the water and wished she could have taken a cooling bath. With luck, Zeke would be coming in a few days, and she wanted to see him again.

Yanyu hurried to the stream and brought a bundle of clothes with her, along with a washboard and small tub. She bowed at Matilda and began to wash clothes. The woman never seemed to talk, so Matilda sat on the bridge and dangled her toes into the water.

She wished she knew how to crochet more than the toes for socks. She wished she knew how to sew. She wished she knew how to make rolls, like Miz Rosalind's. Her wish list was long and she wondered if she'd ever have a chance to learn such things.

Watching Yanyu wash clothing was interesting. The woman made lots of suds using the washboard and when she rinsed everything, the clothes appeared to be very clean. *Maybe I need a washboard? No, I don't. I'm leaving.* Matilda checked her pan and she managed to free the stuck on oats.

Across the way, she spotted a small blackberry bush. Taking her clean pan with her, she retrieved several handfuls of berries. The canes were filled with nasty thorns that cut her hands, arms, and legs. The thorns also snagged her shirt and pants, but the sweet berries were worth the effort. She ate her fill, added more to the pan, and then offered some to Yanyu who smiled and accepted them.

She wanted to go home and read her book, but she was almost afraid to return. Plopping herself on the bridge, she sat there. There was no need for dinner since she'd eaten plenty of berries. Now she kicked herself for not stepping into the soddy long enough to grab the book on American history. She had been reading about Benjamin Franklin and all the things he had done. *If only we had a library here. I'd read everyday.*

That thought mulled in her brain. *Wherever I go I want to work in a library, and if there is no library, I want to start one.* Suddenly, she knew she had a deeper purpose, something specific to do with her life. The concept of being surrounded by books made her spirit soar.

The noon whistle blew. She grabbed her pan and went home. Not wanting to dally, she picked up her book, and returned to town. Finding shade next to the meetinghouse, she sat with her book and reread the part about Benjamin Franklin. She knew she wanted to be a librarian. *If everyone had access to books...*

She read until she heard the afternoon whistle, then a feeling a panic shot through her like icy cold water. She needed to fix supper and have it ready for her family, except she'd lost track of time. At the river's edge, she found several edible greens and picked them. Then she rushed home and dug through the box for whatever food she could find. Normally she would have stopped at the store and bought something in the way of meat, but her brother had bought a pair of boots leaving her with almost no money in her father's account for food. She had stretched what was there as far as it would go. Mr. Jones offered to let her borrow against the upcoming pay period, but she knew not to do that. Finding a few potatoes, an onion, and a can of string beans, she cut up the potatoes into small pieces so they would cook quickly. As soon as they were done she put them into a bowl and placed them in the oven. Then she sliced off a wedge of fatback into her pan, sautéed the onion in the grease until it was soft and golden, stirred in the can of string beans, and added the boiled potatoes, allowing it to cook until the men arrived.

She didn't have long to wait. She could hear them coming, and it was obvious that her brother and father were arguing. Her brother wanted to get away from the mine. He hated living in Homestead Canyon as much as she did. He hated going to the mine and working twelve hours a day, but her father was determined that one day they would have their own strike. *How, when you are working for someone else?*

She put the food into the bowl, brought it inside, placed it by the salad, and set the table.

"This is it?" Her father bellowed at her. "Where's the meat?"

Her insides churned. She looked at her brother briefly and then at her father. "Tomorrow is payday. I'll buy something delicious tomorrow."

"And what about my belly tonight?" He waved his arms through the air. "You give me oats for breakfast and dinner, and you expect me to eat this for supper? I work myself to death in that mine. I need meat."

She stood frozen in place. She didn't want to say that her brother's boots had shorted her for food money. He could have waited to buy new boots, but he wanted them.

"Do you hear me?"

Her body began to tremble. "Yes, Pa. I heard you. I try hard."

"You talkin' back to me?"

"No, sir."

She saw it coming and steadied herself by placing one hand on the table. The sting of her father's hand hitting her face felt like fire, but the real pain came from knowing that her father had hit her.

She stood there for a moment, collecting her wits before she flew out the soddy's door and ran to the stream. Tears flowed over her cheeks. Her father often yelled at her, but she couldn't remember him ever hitting her. Now, she was more determined than ever to get away from Homestead Canyon.

"Matilda." A voice came from behind her. "I'm sorry Pa hit you. He's angry with me. I want to leave here and do something with my life. I'm tired of breathing in brown dust and coughing it out every night. I hate the mine and this town. I want a real job and a wife."

"I'm not staying here any longer than I must. I'm making plans and I have someone helping me. With luck, I'm going to Pennsylvania to stay with a friend's family. We're working on the details for me to travel. Zeke says a female can't travel alone nor can a young boy."

"If I went with you, you wouldn't be alone."

"It's awfully expensive to travel by train. Do you have any money?"

Her brother nodded. "I've been saving my money for something, five dollars a week, the rest goes into Pa's account at the store." He glanced behind him. "I'm sorry about the food money, but I did need the boots."

The morning of payday, she awoke before the mine's whistle and scurried to the privy. That's when she discovered her monthly flow had come. She had overheard her father telling her brother that once he lies with a woman, she could become with child. Wasn't that what she had done with Zeke? They had lain in the grass for quite a while and his kisses had felt wonderful. This was one time she was happy to see the flow.

She returned to her bed and pulled the privacy curtain as she changed her clothes and removed the sheet from her pallet. She needed to wash everything and being she had blood on things, she needed to wash where no one would see her. Her stomach clenched at the thought.

She fixed a breakfast of cornbread baked with berries and fatback drizzled over the top. The inside was moist and the outside was crunchy. She knew her father loved it, but he never once said a word to her. He only grumbled about working and left with an ample amount in his dinner bucket.

After last night, she wanted to go as far away from Homestead Canyon as she could. She replayed the events in her mind as she watched the men leave the soddy. *If my brother would go with me…* Not that she was particularly fond of her brother, but she knew she'd be safe traveling with him.

First, she ran into town and checked with Mr. Jones. He had a long list of deliveries for her to make. If a few of the families gave her a penny for her efforts, she'd have enough money for a toothbrush and for toothpowder. Her toothbrush was worn out and she didn't want to take her father's toothpowder from him.

As she made the deliveries, her thoughts went to the idea of taking her brother with her. *I wonder what Zeke will think of the idea? Please take me away from here.* Then guilt weighed upon her. Mr. Van Dyke had always been so kind to her as had the other residents of the small mining town. And she really did love the little rocky-bottomed stream that had given her so much gold. She stopped for a moment as her mind replayed the beauty that surrounded her. She loved the mountains with the little valley were she played, the plains with its wide-open sky, and Gray Fox. *Oh, no! I can't just leave without telling Gray Fox. He's my friend. What am I going to do? I can't even write to him… unless I tell someone - can't do that…*

Then Miz Della Garfield wanted Matilda to mail a package for her. The package smelled delicious and Matilda knew it contained several bars of soap. *Oh to have such soap!* Then an idea hit. When she finished mailing the package, she returned to Miz Della.

"Um, I was wondering… How much is your soap? The kind that smells good?"

Miz Della frowned. "Why would you want fancy soap?"

Matilda swallowed. "Um, it's not for me. Um, well, it's my brother. He wants a gift for his…"

"Your brother is courting someone?"

"Not exactly. She's, um, they've been, it's a secret. Please don't tell anyone!"

"I won't." Miz Della smiled. "Is it someone here?"

"Oh no. I know he's hoping to see her soon, and he wanted something he could take to her. He was talking about ribbons, but your soaps smell so pretty."

"It's a rather intimate gift for a young man to give her."

"Oh, I think she'd like it. Her family doesn't have much money. I doubt she's ever used such nice soaps."

"My soaps are two cents a bar or three bars for five cents. But maybe he'd prefer something like this." She motioned for Matilda to follow.

In the Garfield kitchen, there were several boxes piled in the corner. Miz Della placed the boxes on the table and opened them.

"These are filled with shavings and a few are filled with broken or imperfect bars. I place them in bags so they can be used in a bath. You don't need to take them out of the bags, but you can if you want. You may have two for a penny."

Matilda stood and sniffed the various bags. Most were labeled with the scent. But one box was filled with bags that had no label. She picked one up and sniffed it. It smelled of pine. The bag was plain and there was no ribbon or lace tying it closed. "This one smells like the woods after a rain."

Della beamed a big grin. "Your brother might like that one for him if he's going a courting. He wants to smell good, too."

"I think you are right." Matilda picked out one for her brother and one for Zeke. Then she started to go through the other two boxes. She fell in love with the one labeled lavender and with the one marked rose, but when she sniffed the one that said gardenia and the one that said magnolia, she knew she wanted them.

Miz Della laughed. "I can tell by the expression on your face that you love our Southern flowers. A family member sends me the oil from those flowers."

Matilda placed the four bags on the table and fished for two pennies in her pocket. "You said two bags for a penny."

Della nodded. "I'll give you this bag for free since you took the package for me and saved me from having to mail it myself."

Matilda picked up the extra bag and sniffed it. "Lavender?"

"Yes. It's nothing but chunks. I had a bar break. Lavender is wonderful for the bath when a woman readies for bed. It's very relaxing, but everyone wants shavings for that. Sprinkle a little baking soda into the bath or a dash of Epsom salts and then wash with lavender. You'll be sleepy in no time." She blushed. "Not that men want to bathe with lavender."

Matilda laughed. *If you only knew Miz Della.* "I'd better head back or Mr. Jones will wonder what happened to me. May I leave them on your back step until I'm done?"

"Certainly."

When she finished her runs, she had six cents. Between that and her tab at the store, she had enough for a fancy toothbrush with a pretty handle and the powder. She left the company store with three cents still in her pocket. After adding it to what she had already saved, she had seven dollars and twenty-eight cents.

Pleased with her savings, she hid her soap, but before closing the lid on that box, she extracted a small sliver from the one that smelled woodsy. She lifted a clean shirt from the shelf over her pallet and some fresh cloth strips that she folded to catch her flow before heading out the door. She had to bathe and wash her other things to remove the blood. Instead of heading to her normal spot, she went further up the stream.

Far in the distance along a ridgeline, she saw horses. There were several bands of wild horses that roamed the area, and they seemed happy to run and frolic. This group didn't look any different.

She knew she had walked a few miles from the town and she was in the wide open. No one could sneak up on her. Dampening the sheet that covered her pallet, she rubbed the bloody spots with her laundry soap, set it to one side, and then did her nightshirt. Washing the dirt from the mine out of clothes was difficult, but washing blood was worse. After several attempts, she managed to get her sheet and nightshirt clean.

The sky over the mountains darkened. The rain was coming, but there was no lightning with it. The stream wasn't very deep here, just a foot or two. She slipped out of her clothes and sat in the water. Using that sliver of soap, she washed her body. The sun still beat down on her and the cool water was refreshing. Leaning her head over her knees, she wet her hair and washed it with that little sliver until there was nothing left of the sliver. She leaned back, closed her eyes to the sun and lay in the water. The sound of rushing water filled her ears. A feeling of being very alive made her body tingle. She thought about Zeke and his kisses, about dresses made of silk and satin, and of tiny shoes to cover her feet. *My long hair perfectly coifed and a dress of the same orange color. Zeke will smile when he sees me.*

The sky darkened above her and she heaved a sigh before opening her eyes. There above her was Merrill Hanson casting a shadow over her. Panic flew through her entire system. His grin was more of a sneer and showed off his stained teeth. She tried to scoot to her feet but he threw himself on her pushing her under the water. Air left her lungs. The water turned icy cold and she fought for the surface. She grabbed a breath before being pushed down again. His hands were squeezing her body. Her lungs burned, as she pushed to the surface again and grabbed another breath. This time he tried to kiss her. She turned her face away from his hot foul breath. His legs were between hers prying them apart and his hand was doing something. His tongue lapped at her ear. Her stomach clenched and she thought she might vomit. This was why her father tried to protect her. She knew what he was trying to do. It was what animals did. *NO!*

Every fiber of her body tightened as she fought to get out from under him. In an attempt to stabilize herself, her hand curled around a small rock. She twisted to the side and using every bit of strength she could muster, brought the rock to his temple. He rolled off of her and she hit him again - this time in the cheek. She heard the crack of the bone and she didn't care. She flipped to her knees and held his face under water. *Dead men can't talk.* She watched the air leave his lungs and the water flow in. *What a filthy bugger!* Blood flowed from his nose, cheek, eyes, and temple.

She heard horses approaching and looked in the direction, her hands were still holding Merrill under the water. She let go of her attacker and screamed, "Gray Fox!"

"What have you done?" He reined his horse to a stop at the water's edge.

"This time I hope I really have killed him."

Gray Fox grinned. "Your freckles cover all of your skin."

She inhaled and ran to the far side of the stream. "Don't look."

"Too late." He laughed. "You are covered in golden fire."

She hurried into her clothing as she listened to more horses approaching. When she turned around she was facing several members of Gray Fox's tribe. She knew most of what they were saying and it wasn't good.

She turned and attempted to smile. "He didn't do it. I did."

Gray Fox was removing the man's clothing. "Make it look as though he was going to take a bath and slipped."

She caught the shirt when Gray Fox tossed it to her.

"Rinse the blood out."

She did as she was told and watched her friend strip the man down to his skin.

"Go home. You not need to know more." Gray Fox's father commanded as he stepped into the water. "We make it look like he fell."

She nodded and began to walk home with wet but clean laundry. Her knees barely carried her. Her entire body shook. It took her over an hour to make the trek, but she knew she needed the time to steady her mind and to organize her feelings. All of her missing pieces about sex came together when she realized what that horrible man was trying to do to her. And her anger towards her father dissipated, as she now understood what her father was trying to do to protect her. If other men in the town knew she was a woman, would she have more of the same? She shuddered at that thought. Zeke was right. She was in danger.

Zeke grimaced. He'd had a long run to make this time with three stops between the stockyard and Homestead Canyon. Lambs were becoming popular. At least Shep kept them moving. *That dog loves to travel and herd.* But the rain made it twice as difficult to maneuver the cart on the rarely traveled road. Had he been on horseback, he would have done better, but chickens required a cart, and carts didn't do well in mud. Rain forced him to stop for the night. Even the chickens settled down and huddled in their cages.

Somewhere through the night, the rain abated, but Zeke was drenched and the cart had sunk into the mud. It took him over an hour to get the wheels moving. He was happy to drop the last of the sheep and most of the chickens at the Ketchem Ranch.

Mrs. Ketchem insisted that he stay long enough to get clean clothes, a warm bath, and food. Normally he would have turned down the offer, but looking his best when he saw Mattie appealed to him. "Thank you, Mrs. Ketchem. Your hospitality is appreciated."

She put a pot of water on the stove. "I'll have that bath ready for you in a few minutes."

By the time he'd finished his bath, he had clean clothes that had been pressed. They were still slightly damp in a few spots. He wasn't certain how she did it, but he was happy to wear them. He joined the family for dinner. The meal was plain but very filling. He especially enjoyed the noodles that had been filled with some sort of potato mixture and fried. The meat was a sausage-like cake that had been sliced and fried. It wasn't as tasty as the scrapple he'd eaten as a child. This was milder but still good. Her rolls were plain, not as yeasty as the Haas' or his mother's. She called them something that sounded like stones.

They had a house full of children, mostly girls, and it was obvious that Mrs. Ketchem was producing more yarn than she could use. But what really impressed him was the house. He'd never seen a log cabin quite like this one.

"Did you build the house?" Zeke asked between mouthfuls.

"Ay, I did. I bought my own saw and cut the lumber." Mr. Ketchem motioned to his wife. "We managed to do it together, but putting the roof on required help which I didn't have. I built it on the ground and used ropes and a couple of oxen to get it up there." He grabbed a child's slate and drew a picture of the situation. "You planning on building one?"

"If I obtain the land I want, I might not have enough leftover for a house, but I'll need one."

"I'm from the Adirondack Mountains, and this area called to my heart. Bet you never heard of the Adirondack Mountains."

"I know where they are. Tucked in the northern portion of the state of New York. Not far from Canada." Zeke laughed. "I happened to like geography."

"So did I. I was topographer with the railroad as they began to survey and make decisions as to where to put the tracks. I thought drawing maps would be exciting. I wanted to do something special with my life. Instead, I discovered I was bored."

The man took another bite of food, chewed, and swallowed. "I came from a farm. We had apple and chestnut orchards to go along with our farm. We worked hard."

"I know about that. I came from a farm outside of Philadelphia. My father would go into Philadelphia several times a week to sell produce."

"I went all the way to California and as I came back, I knew this was where I wanted to be."

"Were you already married?"

Mr. Ketchem shook his head and Mrs. Ketchem answered. "He wrote his mother and asked for a bride. I was twenty-two at the time and still not married." She held up her hands. "Six fingers on each hand. No one wanted me. But my grandmother insisted that I write to Henry. He said he didn't care that I had extra fingers. He was more worried about my being able to move out here and if I could cook. He promised that he was a good man and would treat me well."

Mr. Ketchem chuckled. "I don't mind those extra fingers. She's a hard working woman, and I couldn't ask for a better or prettier wife."

Zeke looked at the dark-haired woman with crystal blue eyes and porcelain white skin and smiled. He wouldn't have called her pretty. He finished his meal and thanked both Ketchums several times before leaving for Homestead Canyon. It was evening when he reached the livery. No one was around. He led the cattle into the paddock and unloaded the six crates of chickens, leaving them by the livery's big door.

He drove through town hoping to catch a glimpse of Mattie, but he also figured she'd be home having supper. As soon as he passed the meetinghouse, he spotted a crowd of people near the tents. He drove onward.

By the bridge, he spotted Mr. Van Dyke. Then he spotted Mattie standing by a man who appeared to be her brother. It was a divided group of people, those who had money and those who didn't. But whatever was going on had brought out the townspeople.

He left his cart by a house and walked the rest of the way. He could hear the people gasping and realized they were walking towards him. That's when he spotted a body on a stretcher. It was naked and bloated like a dead animal that had been left in the sun. Mr. Van Dyke was shouting commands and several of the townsfolk began to disperse.

"Zeke!"

He heard his name but didn't know who called him. Then he saw Mattie. She ran to him and grinned. Her red hair fell in ringlets around her face and bounced with her every move. Next he spotted her bother. Her brother was a larger, heaver version of her. Her brother's hair was shorter and he had a coppery-red mustache to match.

Zeke wanted to collect her into his arms, but he knew not to do that.

She motioned with her hand. "Follow me."

Leaving his cart, he followed her and her brother into a clearing away from the tents and to a northern spot not far from the stream.

The three of them sat in the open area and he wasn't sure why her brother would be present for any conversation that Mattie and he might have. He kept his mouth closed and reckoned he'd listen.

"That was Merrill Hanson. Seems he slipped on some rocks in the stream while bathing." Mattie said looking at Zeke but making an odd expression.

Zeke nodded. "Slipped?" He touched his head at the spot where she'd hit him with a rock. "And hit a rock?"

Mattie touched her fingers to her lips.

Zeke nodded. "I guess all the rain made the water flow faster."

"What rain?" Her brother picked up a handful of dusty dirt.

Zeke lifted his shoulders and let them drop. "I've spent the last three days being drenched. Guess the rain didn't make it over the mountain. Hanover was saturated. My cart became stuck several times."

"Forget about the rain and that bugger. I have something more important to tell you."

Mattie's word choice wasn't lost on him, and he could feel the tingle up his spine. "What?"

"My brother wants to leave here, too. But he only wants to go as far as Philadelphia. He wants a real job of his own."

Zeke looked at the young man beside Mattie and then at Mattie. "Okay, I'm certain that someone from the family will meet you at the Broad Street Station. But I can't afford to send both of you."

"We both have our own money," her brother volunteered.

"It would help if I knew where to go once I was there."

Zeke nodded. "I can ask my parents. When do you want to leave?"

"Tomorrow?" Mattie raised her eyebrows.

Zeke shook his head. "With finding that body… Don't want anyone to think you are running away from trouble."

She wrinkled her nose. "Why would anyone think that?"

Zeke looked at Mattie and touched the scar on his head. "People tend to think the worst of any situation."

"If you won't help us to leave, who will?" her brother asked.

Zeke shook his head. "Let's wait until we know more about that body."

"I don't want to wait." Mattie made a fist and pounded the dirt beside her.

"Mattie, you have to wait. We don't need any suspicion cast on you or your brother."

"Why would anyone look at us?" Mattie's brother asked.

Zeke shrugged. "If they don't figure out a cause of death, they will begin to look for anyone who might have done it. And being you left on the heels of his discovery, they will suspect you."

They watched as several men took off on horseback and followed the stream.

Zeke pointed his finger. "They are looking for answers. Let's wait and see what happens."

Mattie wrinkled her nose and stood. "I need to fix supper for the family."

"Meet me afterwards? I'd like to talk to you."

"Where will I find you?"

He looked around. "The livery. Find the cart."

He walked back to the town, turned the cart around, and headed for the livery. After driving to the side of the building, he moved it to the opposite side. He wanted some privacy and there was none. *Is there any place where I can hold her in my arms and kiss her?*

It was late when Mattie came to the livery. Tucked between the shadow of the livery and his cart, he took her into his arms. "I've missed you. I almost can't stand the thought of sending you to Philadelphia."

"I don't have much time. There's a town meeting tonight." She looked over her shoulder. "They found his boots and his clothing. Now they are trying to decide if he slipped and fell, or if he was murdered."

Zeke took her by her shoulders and held her away from his body. "I want the truth. What happened?"

"I hit him." She began to tremble.

"Was he the one who had been following you?"

"I don't know for certain. I do know that I had done some laundry in the creek and then decided to bathe. I closed my eyes to the sunlight and discovered a shadow instead." She snuffled several times as tears rolled down her cheeks. "Then he was upon me. His hands were… Please don't make me tell you what he did. It was awful."

My poor Mattie, I don't want to ask you, but I must. "Did he enter you?"

She shook her head as more tears slipped down her cheeks.

He drew Mattie to his chest and held her there. "You're

mine, Mattie. No matter what happens to you, you belong to me. I'm the one holding your heart next to mine."

"I killed him before he--"

"He deserved to die." Her tears soaked his shirt, but he didn't care. Her petite body trembled. His heart was breaking to see her this upset. The only thing he could do was hold her tight until her tears stopped.

She pulled away from him and wiped her face on her sleeve.

When he was certain she had composed herself, he turned to the cart. He lifted the package from under the seat of the cart and handed it to her. "I brought you a present but I'm not certain you will like it."

"For me?"

"Travel clothes."

Her excitement waned when she realized what he'd bought.

"Do they fit?"

She held the pants up. "Yes, I believe they will. My brother has never owned such a nice pair of pants."

"And the shirts?"

"Yes."

"Try the shoes."

She slipped them on her feet and took a few steps. "I can put some newspaper in the toes and they will be perfect."

He leaned down. "Do you know how to tie them?"

She huffed. "Yes. I have a brain and all of my fingers."

"Good. You're going to need them when you travel." He stood and looked at her. "Are you comfortable traveling with your brother?"

She nodded. "He's my brother. I'll be fine with him."

Zeke reached into his pocket and pulled out the pouch that he used to hold his money. He extracted several dollars and handed them to her. "This is for your passage. It's enough to take you out there and back. My parents know you are coming. I will send them a telegram when I know you are leaving."

"I don't want to wait."

"You must. I'll send someone next Friday to take you to Hanover." The finality of his words began to choke him. He wrapped her in his arms one more time. "I promise my mother will teach you all the things that you will need to know. And when you are done, I will have a ranch with a proper house for you."

"Please don't forget about me."

"Never. Just the thought of you warms my heart. My soul. I love you, Mattie."

FOUR

Matilda had spent the last few nights tossing and turning, for sleep would not come. Her excitement over leaving Homestead Canyon left her restless. She stood on the platform of Hanover Railroad Station and waited for the train. Her skin prickled with excitement. Her only wish was that she could have dressed like a proper lady, but for the first time in her life that she could remember, she had clean, neat clothes that were brand new. There was even a fancy vest. She wore red suspenders over her blue and white striped shirt. Her brother bought some clothes in Hanover and had changed into them at the bathhouse. Gazing up, she grinned at her brother. *We're a fine-looking set of boys.*

The train blew its whistle and she knew this was it. She thought about her father. At first she thought she'd leave him a note, and then she realized he deserved more than that from her. She told him the evening before they were to leave. He didn't wish her luck or even give her a parting hug. Instead, he asked who would fix his meals. When her brother announced he was leaving, too, her father punched his son, sending the young man into the wall of the soddy. She wound up creating a buffer between her father and brother.

Those days were over and she had a new life. Her brother looked good in his suit and she felt wonderful in her new clothes. She was still hiding as a boy, but it would only be for a few more days. Once she made it to Germantown, Pennsylvania, she would be a proper lady.

The locomotive's whistle blew again. She looked at the carpetbag beside her. It didn't contain much, another set of clothes, writing supplies, her books, and her gold. Homestead Canyon would soon be a distant past. *I'm ready!*

Zeke sent the telegraph to his parents that Mattie was on her way. He promised Mr. Haas that he'd spend the winter at the stockyard and explained that he planned to leave in the spring. But he wanted to at least check out the advertisement for land in Creeds Crossing, Wyoming. Mr. Haas said he was familiar with several ranchers in that area, the Colemans and the McCulloughs. He said they were both producing high quality animals.

Zeke took off on horseback and made the trip in a few

days. The land looked better than anything he'd seen around Homestead Canyon. He called on the McCullough family, being their land bordered what he wanted. Mr. McCullough appeared to be a quiet man. He was neither friendly nor forthcoming, but Zeke was given the impression that Mr. McCullough was honest.

Zeke did find out that he couldn't depend on the river or the streams to provide water in the hot summer months. But after riding the property, Zeke found a gully that he could dam and create an excellent lake. There was good grazing land. It wasn't the rich loam he'd had growing up, but it appeared as though the land was reasonably fertile for crops, which pleased him. There was also a healthy wooded area that would yield him plenty of timber for building and for heating. He went to the land office and gave the railroad his offer. The only thing left for him to do was to wait for their reply.

He tried not to raise his hopes, but he had no reason to believe that he wouldn't be able to purchase the property. His concern was the cost. He didn't know there were added fees. The land office informed him of those fees when they took his down payment and placed his offer. The added amount would wipe Zeke out. He knew he could cut his own timber, but it would take longer, and that still didn't leave him enough to afford nails. He didn't want to have to borrow from his dad. His dad believed that you saved until you could afford something or you did without.

Zeke knew he'd have to be very careful with the money he was earning. Still, it wouldn't be enough. The longer it took the longer he'd be separated from Mattie. *I hope I haven't made a huge mistake.*

The train jostled Matilda until she was certain that her insides would be scrambled. She lost her appetite. Nothing much appealed to her and her brother pushed her aside.

He made it quite clear that he didn't want to hear her complaints or be bothered.

They stopped in a small town and everyone went to have a meal at the restaurant. But as she walked the short distance, she could feel the revulsion in her stomach. It felt as though her stomach had been turned upside-down, shaken, and as though it were a pot ready to boil over. She asked her brother if he would bring her plain coffee and a biscuit.

"If you want something, you'll manage like everyone else."

"Please?"

"Get it yourself. You're not a baby."

She forced herself to walk down the dirt street, and through the door of the restaurant.

"Oh, my dear boy, you must have motion sickness. You've turned the color of new grass sprouts in the spring." A woman in a white apron ushered Matilda to a table by a side door. "Let me give you some tea that will help settle your stomach."

Matilda nodded.

The woman brought a hot cup of tea that had been sweetened with plenty of honey, but the honey was there to cover the taste of something bitter. Matilda couldn't quite place what was added, but she continued to sip on the tea, trusting the woman who probably saw plenty of passengers who also discovered that riding a train jumbled their innards.

Matilda soon realized she was getting sleepy. The woman returned to the table and handed Matilda a jar of tea and several rolls wrapped in paper.

"Sip your tea and enjoy the rolls. You'll feel better soon. How far are you traveling?"

"The Philadelphia area of Pennsylvania."

"Oh, my, you'll do better in a few days. You grow accustomed to it. Look out the window at distant objects." The woman patted Matilda on the shoulder. "You'll be fine, sonny. Give yourself a chance."

Unsure how she'd make it back to the train's car, Matilda paid the required three cents and forced herself to return. The car was empty. She curled up on her seat and quickly fell asleep. In the vague recesses of her mind, she remembered hearing the train's whistle, and the noise of the other passengers, and feeling the car move.

When she opened her eyes, it was almost dark outside. She ate a bit of a roll and drank some of the tea in the jar. Then she went back to sleep and repeated that scenario several times until morning broke. A war had raged between her head and her stomach, but they must have signed a truce while she slept.

She stared out the window. Everything looked different, greener and flatter. The train's whistle blew and they pulled into another town. This morning, she was starved. The restaurant had a simple menu of pancakes and eggs. Having never eaten a pancake, she wondered what it was and why would anyone eat cake for breakfast? She devoured the meal, wrote a short letter to Zeke, and managed to mail it before the train left the station.

The train had another stop in a larger town and there Matilda found a mine exchange company. With several tiny gold nuggets in her pocket, she decided to see if she could discover their worth. She pushed open the door to the small building.

"Hello." She withdrew a small nugget and handed it to the man behind the counter. "Can you help me with this?"

"I'll do my best. That's why I am here." He took the odd shaped ball and examined it. "May I ask where you found it?"

"Wyoming, in a stream."

He did several things including weighing it and gave her a price.

She furrowed her brow. "How do I know you're not cheating me?"

He pointed to a certificate. "You don't. But if I cheat you, I'd lose my license." He withdrew a slip of paper from under the counter. "Here's your weight and here's the value. Our government determines the value of gold." He pointed to a figure on the page. "And I keep a percentage."

She raised her eyebrows. "What if I have more?"

"How much more? I don't have too much cash, but I can write you a check that you can deposit in any bank."

Satisfied that he was telling her the truth, she smiled and held out her hand.

The clerk dropped her little ball into it.

"I'll be back, with the rest of it."

She grabbed her carpetbag from the train and returned to the mine exchange. Very carefully, he weighed all the pieces except for those in her pocket. As he wrote down the weight and calculated the amount, she did the math in her head behind him. She was about to go from poor to extremely wealthy in a matter of minutes. "How do I know that the check you give me will be good?"

He chuckled. "Would you like me to go with you to the bank?"

"I want cash."

At the bank, it took a few minutes to count the cash and hand it over. Never had she'd seen so much money or possessed that much. She packed it into her carpetbag and dashed for the train.

Her brother asked her what she was doing.

"I was curious. You and Pa mined copper all day long. I wondered what happened to it."

When they pulled into Chicago, her heart raced. She and her brother disembarked and went to the ticket booth. The next train left in the morning and they were told that they needed to spend the night at a hotel. Her brother huffed off, leaving her to fend for herself.

Zeke had given her money, but she didn't want to spend it for anything other than train fare. After wandering around the city and looking at all the tall buildings, she was certain that she'd have a crick in her neck.

Afraid that she might wander into a saloon, she looked in the windows before settling on a small restaurant. She looked at the menu and had no idea what to order. A young woman came over and asked if she had money.

"Yes. I can pay for my meal." She produced several coins and showed the woman. "But I do not know what to eat. I do not know these foods."

The woman cocked her head. "Do you eat cooked tomatoes?"

"Tomatoes? What are they?"

The woman laughed. "I'll bring you some spaghetti. You will like it."

A few minutes later, the woman returned with a dish filled with stringy-looking white things with something red on it that had something sprinkled all over it.

Matilda stuck her fork into the dish and scooped up something that she thought was impossible to eat.

The woman giggled and showed her how to twirl what she called noodles onto the fork. It took Matilda several tries to get something that she could fit into her mouth. But once she tasted it, she loved it. She ate the entire dish and asked for more.

"Let me bring you something slightly different."

This time, the noodles were flat and there was meat mixed into the sauce. Matilda ate all of it, paid for her meal, and left for the train station.

She had wandered further than she realized and was totally lost. After asking for directions twice, she eventually returned to the station. Using her carpetbag as a pillow, she curled into a ball on a bench and fell asleep.

She awoke to her brother standing over her. "There are jobs here. Lot's of them."

Taking the newspaper from him, she read several listings.

"Are you leaving me to travel alone?"

"You don't need me. I can find a real job here and make plenty of money."

"But I thought you were going to look in Philadelphia for a job?"

"I don't need to do that when there are plenty here."

She rolled her eyes at her brother. "Very well, leave me. I can survive without you."

The thought of traveling alone gripped her insides, yet she also felt as though he'd not been the least bit helpful along the way. She watched him walk away. Having been told they were two peas in a pod, she knew that wasn't true, for she would have never left a younger brother or sister to fend for him or herself.

Sadness mixed with anger. She had left her father, but her brother walked away from her. They were her family, all that she had known, and now they were gone. She was alone, but hadn't she always been alone? Then she thought about Zeke.

Part of her wanted to write to Zeke and tell him what her brother had done, but she knew that would be upsetting. *I can do this. Train travel is very easy.*

She caught her train to New York. This time she didn't dare get off until she had to switch trains. After eating a sausage-like thing called a hot dog for six cents from a vendor at the station, she caught the train to Philadelphia's Broad Street Station.

How would anyone know who she was or how would she know Zeke's family? She wandered around and eventually the crowd thinned. The noisy locomotives and the smoke that fill that station made her want to gag, yet she was starving. On a bench sat a woman and two girls, they were nicely dressed and all of them were blondes, not unlike the color of Zeke's hair.

Collecting a little courage, Matilda approached them. "Hello, I'm looking for Zeke Hillerman's family."

The woman shook her head, and Matilda's heart sank. Had she traveled this far for nothing? She found a bench and sat on it. She was determined not to cry. *I need to make plans.*

After sitting there for several minutes, an unfamililar man approached with a teen boy. "Excuse, me, I'm looking for Matt from Wyoming."

Matilda jerked her head up at the man. "Who are you?"

"Why don't you tell me your name first?"

"My last name is Berwyn. I'm supposed to meet Mrs. Hillerman."

The man smiled. "Zeke is my son. You're a day late. My wife came yesterday."

Zeke returned to the Haas stockyard and discovered several letters from Mattie. He was excited about the possible land purchase, yet the fact that it would leave him almost penniless weighed on him. He went back to work with gusto, assuming that work would keep his mind off Mattie's absence and his lack of funds.

The following week another letter arrived from Mattie saying that she was with his family. She also told of her brother's departure in Chicago. Anger over her brother's negligence washed through him, but he was relieved Mattie was safe. He knew he shouldn't have doubted her ability to take care of herself, but he was raised to protect the women around him. *I should have gone with her.*

He promised himself that he'd take time tonight and write to her, but he had over two hundred head of cattle coming, and they all had to be weighed.

Matilda shared a room with Zeke's sister Priscilla and received several dresses to wear that had belonged to Miriam, Zeke's next to the youngest sister. They weren't the fancy dresses she'd seen Lena wear, but they were still pretty. These clothes were plainer. No longer did she need to bind her breasts, but instead of it feeling good, they hurt. Then she discovered that acting like a lady meant she couldn't run barefoot, much less run, and even through the warmth of the day, she was covered in a long dress and expected to do chores.

She was also used to be being by herself and not having someone telling her what to do and when to do it. She couldn't take off and explore the countryside around her. A feeling of being trapped enclosed her. Yet there was so much to learn.

The Hillerman's had real silverware and she had to learn where each piece went when she set the table. Nor did she realize it was supposed to be held a certain way. There was so much to remember and it was so easy to forget. Her foot went into the hem of her skirt and she fell on her way up the stairs.

After what Matilda decided was the most frustrating week in her life, she begged for some time to wander the farm. The further she walked from the house the more she liked what she saw. Rolling hills were blanketed in a patchwork of crops or were covered in green grass and contained everything from horses to pigs. Several creeks cut through the valleys and in the distance she could see several other houses.

She could hear a horse approaching from behind her and turned to see who was coming. It was Joshua, Zeke's brother who was close to her in age. He waved a greeting and pulled his horse next to her.

"Is everything all right?" Josh asked, sounding very much like his older brother.

She nodded and then laughed. "It's horrible and wonderful all rolled into one."

He knitted his brow.

"I've always wanted to wear dresses." She wrinkled her nose. "But they are hot and uncomfortable. Your mother's cooking is delicious, yet I can't seem to get the fork from the meat to my mouth the proper way."

"You're doing fine."

"No, I'm not. I overheard your mother saying I was a waif with absolutely no home training, and she can't figure out why Zeke cares about me."

Josh laughed. "Well, it's obvious that you've never had any training, but you'll learn."

"No one told me not to use my fingers or to close my mouth

when I chewed. I understand. I really do. I'm not stupid. But I've been on my own since I was younger than your baby sister Esther. My dad went to work in the mines and I stayed home. It was my job to do the cooking and the cleaning. But I ran free most of the time."

"Sounds like fun."

"It was also boring. Other people had things to do. I'd do my work and then play."

There was rustling in the grass near them and Matilda turned to see what it was. She watched the spot and then saw the tail. Touching her fingers to her lips with one hand, she reached in her pocket with her other and withdrew her little knife. A moment later, she confirmed what it was and tossed her knife.

Josh gasped.

"It's dead." She walked to the spot, and picked up the rodent with her knife embedded in it. After pulling the knife out, she almost wiped the blade on her dress. Instead she wiped it in the grass and then on the bark of a nearby tree before placing it in the buffalo leather sheath that Gray Fox had given her.

"You killed that rat from at least twenty feet away. That's amazing."

"What is?"

"That you could throw a knife that far and hit a moving target."

She raised her eyebrows and shook her head. "Don't tell me that you don't learn to do such things on a farm."

He swallowed. "No."

"What do you do when you have a rattlesnake or something?"

"Rattlesnake? We don't have anything like that. Maybe a garter snake occasionally, but the chickens will kill it. Seems they don't take to snakes."

"Snakes eat their eggs." Mattie frowned.

"These snakes are too small to eat anything that large. They eat bugs."

"Maybe the chickens don't know that."

Josh laughed. "Little difficult to explain it to them."

"I don't belong here. I wanted to learn to be a lady and wear pretty dresses, but I realize I'll never be that kind of person."

"Why do you say that?"

She shrugged and walked away. "Because I can kill a rodent." *Or a man.*

Josh caught up to her. "Follow me. I have something to show you."

They walked across the grassy field where several sheep grazed. When they were at the top of the small rise, she felt as though she could see forever.

Josh put his hands on her shoulders and turned her. "See? Over there? That's Philadelphia."

"Are those the masts of ships that I see?"

"Yes. They are on the Delaware River. And do you see that tall building? That will be our city hall. When it's done, there will be a statue of William Penn on the top of it, and it will be the tallest building in the world." He pointed to an area away from the city. "That's Germantown. And the school is right there, slightly hidden by the trees."

"When do I go to school?"

Josh frowned. "It starts in two weeks. Sometimes Mr. Schumacher will give us a lift. Otherwise, we walk."

"That's the best news I've heard since I arrived."

"I think you have birds in your belfry."

"My belfry is fine. I am going to be a librarian." She turned and this time walked to the house.

As she stepped through the back door, Mrs. Hillerman smiled. "Matilda how was your afternoon?"

"Very good, ma'am. I was able to see the ships on the river."

"Oh, my, you walked quite a distance to be able to see them. That rise is at the far end of our property."

"It was nothing to walk that far. I used to walk that sometimes just to bathe in the creek."

"You'd bathe in the creek?"

"Except in the winter, but carting enough water for a bath…" She giggled. "Sometimes I'd skip bathing and just use a wash rag because it was too cold in the soddy."

"What is a soddy?"

Matilda looked at the woman as she tried to decide how to best explain it. "It was my home. It's made of sod. You find some grassy land and then cut squares of it." She held her hands apart to show the size. "And stack them. Ours was covered with a tin roof and more sod on top of that. Then the dirt floor is coated in blood, which makes it shiny and easy to keep clean." Matilda watched Mrs. Hillerman's face turn ashen. "The whole soddy was probably this much of your kitchen." She extended her arms to show off the square footage. We had a Franklin stove there, and I had a pallet there with a curtain. My brother slept there, and my father there. With a small table there and three logs for seats."

"That's it?"

Matilda nodded, and then squared her shoulders. "I kept the soddy clean, kept our clothes clean, and made the meals. The rest of the time I was free to roam the countryside."

"No one watched over you?"

Matilda shrugged. "Who would do that? My father and brother worked from six in the morning until six at night." She grinned. "I did have a playmate. A Lakota Sioux Indian would often be in the area and I'd sneak off with him and even went to his encampment and spent time with his mom."

"You played with a savage?"

"Of course. His mother was so nice to me. She taught me to make cornbread and to do all sorts of things. I even know how to skin a rabbit."

"You are lucky they didn't skin you."

"Why would you say that?"

"Because they are savages. They scalp people."

Matilda stared at the woman before her. "They had no reason to hurt me. I played with their son, Gray Fox."

"Enough." Mrs. Hillerman waved her hands in front of her face. "No more talk of savages." She turned away and called, "Priscilla, I want you and Matilda to choose a chicken for dinner."

Priscilla entered the kitchen and frowned. "I hate trying to catch one. Why can't Miriam do it?"

"Because I want her to peel potatoes."

Priscilla looked at Matilda and frowned. "Do you know how to catch a chicken?"

Matilda followed her roommate outside and watched as she tried to catch a young rooster. After several minutes of observing Priscilla running after a chicken, Matilda called for Priscilla to stop. Matilda withdrew her knife from her pocket. "That one with the feather that's standing up?"

Priscilla nodded.

Matilda raised her knife and let it fly. The neck was severed as the knife made contact.

Priscilla gasped.

Matilda collected the chicken and began to remove the feathers. It didn't take her long to strip the bird naked. Holding the chicken by the feet, she carried it into the house and set it down on the table in the kitchen. She looked at Mrs. Hillerman. "Anything else?"

Priscilla stepped into the kitchen. "Mama!"

Zeke opened his letter from Matilda. It was both sad and funny for she talked about sleeping in a room with Priscilla and wearing Miriam's hand-me-downs. His family was not poor nor were they wealthy. The farm was successful and his father took a cart filled with vegetables into Philadelphia three days a week. Once a month, Zeke's mom would go with her husband and sell her yarn to a few specialty stores.

They didn't lack for anything, but nothing was abundant. They had an ordinary home. Not much different from any of the other homes in the area. Built with stone, it was two stories high with dormer windows in the attic. A big chimney marked each of the four corners of the house and carried away the smoke from four large downstairs stoves. Three were for heat, and one was for cooking. On extra cold nights, his father would light the two stoves upstairs to keep everyone from freezing to death while they slept. Apparently Zeke's two eldest brothers and their wives had taken over the attic and created their own living spaces up there.

He could understand Mattie's awe over the simplest of things. To her, the Hillerman house was a palace, and sleeping in a proper bed was something she had never experienced. He remembered Priscilla's room. It was wallpapered in green with tiny white flowers. Her pitcher and basin matched her wallpaper and the two narrow beds in her room were canopied. *As much as Priscilla loves me, she must be happy to have Mattie staying in the room with her.*

In his mind's eye, he could see his family's house as clearly as if he were standing in it. He remembered the day he and his brothers moved the old parlor furniture to the attic and his mom had her new set delivered. It was royal blue and gold. The chairs were covered in a pale golden fabric with vibrant birds of paradise printed on it and the sofas were royal blue with gold trim. Every piece had large curved and rounded edges.

His mother had been so excited that she was almost in tears. It was the latest style, and he knew it had cost his father a fortune. But his dad said she deserved it. That was a year before Zeke left to make his own way in the world. Now Matilda was telling him everything about the house as if he'd never seen it.

He laughed to himself when she began to describe the dresses. Miriam had heavier bones and was much younger than Mattie, but by now was probably much taller than Mattie. For she was like a tiny bird compared to his sisters.

He laughed when he read how she killed the chicken and how amazed Priscilla was at Mattie's skill. Mattie didn't have to explain how she had learned to wield a knife. He figured Gray Fox had taught her.

The following morning another letter came for him. His land purchase had been denied. The land was already sold. He swallowed the lump that formed in his throat as he continued to read. The railroad offered him another piece. It wasn't as large and it was tucked against the south end of the town. It was half the size, but all fertile land, and the price was much less. He had ten days to respond and he couldn't remember if it had a stream.

"Mr. Haas? May I have a word with you?"

"Certainly. Have you received bad news? I thought a letter from the railroad would put a smile on your face."

He held the letter in one hand and rolled the palm up of the other. "I didn't get the land, but they've offered me another piece. I have ten days to respond."

"Where's this second piece of land?"

"South of the other piece. If I remember correctly it's grazing land, but I don't know if it has water on it."

Mr. Haas shook his head. "You don't want land without water."

"I know that's what I was thinking. I hate to ask if I can take off again with such short notice, but…" Zeke held his breath.

"Never buy a pig in a poke. You need to check that land. Is the price the same?"

Zeke shook his head. "There are less acres, quite a bit less, but I think it's better land."

"You need to check it carefully. This is the worst time of the year for you to leave. We have a few hundred head of cattle coming in here tomorrow. After that, the numbers will be much smaller, but I really need you to handle the chute. No one else is as good or as quick as you are with the animals."

"May I leave after that?"

Mr. Haas nodded. "I know how important the land is to you." Then he smiled. "Have you heard from your young woman?"

Zeke gave him a smile. "I think my mother has her hands full. Mattie is rather independent and not the least bit genteel."

Mr. Haas chuckled and motioned with his thumb. "My wife would never make it on a ranch."

The following morning, Zeke was coping with over eight hundred head of cattle. One of Wyoming's largest ranches sent stock to be sold at market. He stood on a wooden rail of the chute and began to weigh and mark each animal's weight as it came through the chute. Clay stood behind Zeke recording the weights in a book.

Out of the corner of Zeke's eye he realized that one steer was balking at going into the chute and the cowboys had used a prod on him. When he reached the scale, Zeke looked at the steer that had a large wad of salvia hanging from his mouth. "Come on, big boy, you're next."

He reached down and took the steer by the nose and dragged him onto the scale. "Fifteen twenty-one. You are a big boy!"

Zeke dipped his paintbrush into the can of paint and climbed up the rail to paint the steer's weight on his side. He awakened a few seconds later on the ground and his leg burning with pain.

FIVE

Zeke seemed to swing from being alert to being in pain and passing out. He was loaded on the train and sent to Hanover. Only bits and pieces of time and places stayed with him as though it were all a dream. But when he opened his eyes and had no pain, panic ran through him faster than an icy gust from the north. He pulled himself off the pillow enough to assure himself that he still had a leg. Wrapped and bandaged, it was there.

Someone would occasionally wake him and give him water and broth before he slipped into another dream of horses running amuck, bulls charging him, dead animals, or Indians threatening Mattie. He was at the point where he didn't want to fall asleep. Each dream was another nightmare. He tried to stay awake, but a million black bugs crawled up the walls and over his sheets.

"Ezekiel, calm down. It's your medication. There's nothing here." A dark-haired man in a starched white shirt with a wide, folded flat collar patted Zeke's arm. "I'm going to back you off your medicine, but you'll feel the pain of your leg."

"I can handle the pain."

The man chuckled. "You cowboys are all the same. You think you can handle anything."

"Please don't go away. Talk to me."

The man patted his arm. "You're not the only patient."

A few moments later, a woman walked into the room. She was probably the same age as his mother.

"Don't like being alone, eh?" She pulled up a chair and began to knit. "Where are you from, young man?"

"Back east, near Philadelphia. My family has a farm there."

Her needles clicked together at a constant speed. "Why didn't you stay there? Did you run away?"

"No." He could feel himself trying to drift off into another dream. "I have two older brothers. They will inherit the farm. I needed my own…"

He opened his eyes and there was the woman smiling at him.

"Ready for some breakfast?"

"Coffee?" His voice was hoarse.

She handed him a simple glazed cup and he tasted it. Honey sweetened, it was delicious. He swigged it down and asked for another cup.

"Why don't you eat a little something?" She put a tray in front of him as he sat up.

He inhaled deeply and held it for a few seconds. "Oh, pain!"

She twittered. "You've been raised well. I've heard many a curse word, but good boys don't curse."

"Thanks, but I'd like to let loose with every curse word I know, except you're standing in the room."

"I'll tell you a secret. Cursing doesn't make the pain go away. It doesn't do a thing."

"I'd still like to curse."

She twittered again like the trill of small bird. "Eat your breakfast. I didn't make it to have it go to waste."

The woman reminded him of Cook. Except this woman had graying, light brown hair that was pulled into a tidy bun.

He ate his egg and the roll, but he wasn't so certain about the piece of meat. "Can you save this for me." He pointed to the slice of ham. "I'm not sure I'm ready to eat it."

He slid his hand over his belly as a wave of nausea washed through him.

"Ready for the coffee?"

"Now, I'm… It's a little rocky in there."

"That's your pain medicine wearing off." She fixed him a cup and handed it to him. "You'll be fine. Food will help the feeling to go away. An empty stomach will allow the sensation to linger longer."

"Oh. Thank you." He took the cup and looked at it before setting it on the table beside him.

She took his tray and disappeared through a doorway.

Another wave of nausea washed over him. He leaned against

the headboard of the bed and waited for it to end, wondering where he was and how long he'd been there. In the distance, he heard a train whistle, but he had no sense of direction. Was the sound coming from the east or the west? He wanted to ask. He closed his eyes and waited for someone to return to his room.

Memories of being little and sick flowed through his mind. His mom would tuck him in bed and make him stay there. He remembered being covered in an itchy rash that was weepy and sore to touch, and only his older sister, Ruth, was allowed to come into his room. She read a book of poems to him and another story about a kitten.

He wasn't allowed to call for things. His mother made it quite clear that she had more to do than hold his hand. She handed him a slate and told him to practice his numbers. That same bored feeling weighed on him.

In another room, he could hear hushed voices, but he couldn't discern what was being said. He blew out a breath and looked at his toes sticking out of the bandages. They looked purplish and slightly swollen. From the way the leg was wrapped with wooden slats, he was certain he'd broken it.

He remembered the one steer that had been prodded. He wasn't going to hurt the steer, but the scared creature didn't know that. But what exactly happened, he couldn't recall. *What day is it?*

He reached for his coffee. It was barely lukewarm. The train whistle blew again and he could hear the train stopping nearby. *I must see that land or I won't be able to purchase it. They gave me ten days.*

The feeling of being trapped shrouded him and left him coping with depression. *There's other land.* He thought about the green grassy areas he'd seen and the gentle slopes and gullies. He thought about the house that he wanted to build and the fir trees in the area. *Mattie, my sweet Mattie.*

The voices in the other room fell silent.

The doctor appeared. "Hello. How are you feeling?"

"As long as I don't move my leg, I'm fine. Other than that, I have some nausea."

"You ate your breakfast. That is a good sign." The doctor touched several places on his leg.

"Damnation! What are you doing to me?" His hands fisted the sheets, as pain ripped through him. When the stars before his eyes cleared, he asked, "What was wrong? And will I heal completely?"

"You broke it in two places. I had to reset the bone and to do that required surgery. In another week, I'll take the stitches out. Behave yourself and I might let you out of bed tomorrow."

"I can't stay that long. I need to go to Creed's Crossing."

The doctor shook his head. "You must stay put if you want the leg to heal correctly. I never saw such a mess."

"Am I going to be a cripple?"

Mattie went to school a few days early to talk with the teacher. She'd never seen such a large school. Pulling open the heavy front door, she blinked as she entered the building. The place smelled of pine oil. There was no one in the office so she wandered the halls until she found a teacher.

"Oh, I'm sorry, I teach third grade. You want Miss Pritchard. She is on the other side on the second floor. I saw her earlier so I'm certain she's here. Was she expecting you?"

"No, ma'am." Matilda curtsied and quickly left. The upper bustled with activity and she finally found Miss Pritchard.

"Hello. I'm Matilda Berwyn and I'd like to take my final exams."

Miss Pritchard smiled and extended her hand. "Pleased to meet you, Miss Berwyn. Can you tell me why have you not taken your final exams?"

Mattie sucked in a breath. "My father moved the family and there was no school. My last exam was for the eighth grade. I took it when I was nine."

Miss Pritchard raised her eyebrows. "Do you have that certificate?"

"Yes, ma'am, but I didn't bring it with me today. I'll bring it to you tomorrow. I didn't know you would need it." As her body tensed, her words came out faster. "I'm leaving again in the spring and I want to be a librarian. I thought it was best if I proved my worthiness with my final exam certificate."

"I hate to disappoint you, but librarians study the arts in college before taking on such a job."

"I don't have time for that." She squared her shoulders and tried to remember everything Mrs. Hillerman had said about a lady's posture. "There is no library where I'm going. I'm going to start one."

"That's very admirable. But what makes you think you can just take your final exam?"

"Oh, I thought I might have to read a few things first, and I'd like to know what books they might be."

"Miss Berwyn, my job is to prepare my pupils for college, to be certain they have the skills they need to become productive members of society. You will be placed in the ninth grade class if you can prove that you took your eighth grade exams."

"But I have always worked ahead. My last school only had two teachers. It was easy to work ahead, and when I wasn't doing that, I was helping to teach."

"Here you will stay in your classroom and do the same work as your classmates." She folded her arms over her chest. "Your teacher will be Miss Schwartz."

"Thank you, ma'am." Matilda dropped another curtsy and tried not to run from the building. *Why can't she understand?*

Her anger and frustration waned as she walked to the Hillerman's farm, but her disappointment wouldn't go away. *If I can do the work, why can't I take the exam?*

The following day she took her certificate back to the school and it was duly recorded in her records. But the principal, Mr. Geiger, also wanted her parents' signature on several forms.

"My mother died when I was young and my father is in the Wyoming Territory. Up until a few weeks ago, that's where I lived with him, and I can tell you it is still Indian hunting grounds. I'm here to learn farming, cooking, and other important skills from the Hillerman's. I was hoping I'd be able to take my final exam before I left this spring."

Mr. Geiger huffed. "What makes you think you can take the exam?"

She smiled as sweetly as she could muster under the circumstances. "Because someone will tell me what I will need to know. If I need help with anything, I will ask."

"You think that's all there is to school?"

She shrugged. "I already told Miss Pritchard that I was allowed to work at my own speed, and when I wasn't working, I was helping the children below me."

"That's not how we do it here. You will be placed in the ninth grade classroom. You will have more than enough to learn."

"But what about all the things I've learned on my own, the books that I've read, and the mathematics I've used."

"You will be placed in the ninth grade. Tell Mrs. Hillerman I need her to sign your forms, since she's acting as your mother."

Matilda raised her eyebrows. "Since you are ordering me around and acting like an overbearing father, you sign them."

She stood, nodded her head, and turned. Her yellow dress made a swishing sound and that pleased her even more.

Under the law she wasn't required to attend school. She had her certificate of completion of the eighth grade and she had passed with the highest possible marks. Her teacher was so proud of her and her father hardly said more than she had done well. Now she was facing a school that wanted to treat her as a child. *I'm not going there!*

Matilda tried to explain everything to Mrs. Hillerman, but the woman swore that school was the best option. There was a country schoolhouse a few miles in the opposite direction.

Matilda would never get the same education there.

Being short had worked to Matilda's advantage in Homestead Canyon, but it was hurting her in Germantown. Dressed in a pretty blue dress with a bustle and certain her shoes were shined as bright as possible, she was pleased with appearance. She refused to pack a dinner bucket. There was no way she would starve and if she was hungry, there was a neglected apple tree on the school grounds. She dug through the large wardrobe and found a lace shawl.

Priscilla looked at her and gasped. "This is school, not a debutante ball."

Matilda stuck out her chin as she tossed the shawl around her shoulders. "I know that, and I'm not about to be treated like a child."

She did everything she could to maintain her posture and composure as she walked into the school. In her assigned classroom, she took a seat in the back. It was all she could do to stay awake, and she wished she had brought her writing supplies with her. She could have used the time to write to Zeke.

When she heard her name, she looked at the teacher. "I'm sorry, ma'am. What was your question?"

"We will be studying the Civil War and I asked your opinion of slavery." Miss Schwartz smiled, but it looked more like a sneer.

Matilda raised her eyebrows. "Considering this area is the vocal home of the abolitionists. What do you expect me to say?"

"But I asked *your* opinion of slavery."

Matilda rose from her seat. "The color of our skin does not

make us superior. The Civil War was not fought over slavery. It was fought over economics, which happened to include slavery. So now we employ cheap, Negro labor. We fail to pay them enough to make a living, but we no longer own them. So all is well in the world? Not really. It's not much different from the way we've treated the Chinese who have built our railways, yet it's definitely better than what we've done to our Indians. We are doing everything we can to destroy our Indians by removing them from their land, preventing them from hunting, and allowing them to starve or freeze to death. And as for the Negroes, I see them in this area, but I don't see a single pupil in this school who is a Negro. People need to look at the bigger picture. Does that answer your question?"

She returned to her seat and stared out a window. *As my father would say, let her chew on that.*

She half listened to what the teacher was saying and heard Miss Hersheimer ask, "Matilda, since you seem to have formed a strong opinion and having grown up west of the Mississippi River, would you care to enlighten us on the effect of the Civil War on those territories?"

"The war ended quite a few years before I was born. Even my father was a small child at the time. I do know from what some of the older people have said that the war was simply something everyone read about in stale newspapers. It slowed the progression of the railroad, for they had to rebuild before they could go west. For most of those living west of the Mississippi, the war was a major monetary delay. But the East, prior to the war, was not as reliant on beef and wheat production as they are now. So what was an annoyance to those in the West later became a boon to those struggling to carve a living in the territories." She stared at the teacher who was probably only a few years older than she. "The railroads are making it easy for those in the West to ship products."

Maybe she hadn't had many books to read over the last few years, but she'd had sheets of newspaper filled with news and politics. At the time, she thought it was a curse and now she saw it as a blessing.

She sat through the morning lessons until it was time for dinner. Several of her classmates walked home. She walked into the sunshine and found a bench under a tree. *Why can't I just take my exam? Why must I be this bored?*

After the recess, she joined her classmates for yet another tedious session. This time it was science and mathematics being taught by Mr. Bickers. When a classmate asked virtually the same question for the third time and received the same answer, Matilda had enough. She felt sorry for her classmate Carl who was struggling to understand.

She stood and stared at the teacher. "Excuse me, sir. May I explain it?"

"You think you can teach this class for me?"

"I have no desire to teach your class, but you seem to be missing the basic premise of his question." She turned to her classmate. "Numbers aren't always physical. We have to account for the things that aren't there but should be." She glanced at the teacher. "If you went to the store and bought six… nails, except when you returned home and opened the package there were only five. How do you count something that isn't? In your mind, you know there is a missing nail, but you can't count it." She continued to explain. "Think of the number line not as a yardstick, but as a ribbon in the air. It doesn't have a beginning or an end. It goes forwards and backwards and allows us to count in each direction. We don't have to really understand how it could be there, we only need to accept that it exists and that it allows us to find answers." She took a breath and kept going. "Once you take geometry, you'll discover that there are circles and planes. They don't exactly exist. They are only theories because if they were one molecule thick then they would exist as a three-dimensional object. You'll also discover that everything isn't perfect. If you have a pie and you want to share it with two friends, you will never be able to cut that pie into three pieces the exact same size. Someone will receive a slightly larger cherry. Thirty-three and a third times three will never count up to one hundred percent, there's a one tenth of one that's unaccounted, and that one tenth can be divided by three until we can no longer see to divide it. And that's why we have this theoretical ribbon in the sky and not a yardstick." She took a deep breath and continued about how many kernels of corn would fit in a silo. "So it's all theoretical, because no one is actually going to count how many pieces of corn are in there."

"Thank you, Miss Berwyn. That was an excellent explanation. Does anyone else have any questions or may I continue?"

The following morning, she walked to school with Zeke's siblings, but as she stepped into the building, she was called to the office, where Mr. Geiger, the principal, was waiting for her.

"Just how much mathematics have you had?"

She shrugged. "There was an older boy where I used to go to school, and I was always doing mathematics with him."

"Have you studied Shakespeare?"

"Who?"

"Jonathan Swift?"

She shook her head while the principal named several more people.

She and Mr. Geiger had a lively discussion, and in the end, it was decided that she lacked books and Pennsylvania history. Mr. Geiger walked her down a hallway and found her a book to read.

He ushered her in a room. "Read this, and when you are done, bring it to me. I will then give you another."

And what did I tell you last week? She smiled to herself. *I have other things to learn.*

Zeke was given crutches, but the pain in his leg continued and the doctor decided on more surgery. The days ticked by and Zeke knew he'd lost the land that he wanted. Now he'd have a medical bill to pay and even less money. His dreams were shattered. The thought of writing to Mattie and telling her that he had failed, stabbed at him. He had to get well enough to return to his job, if he still had a job.

He was eating his breakfast when Mr. Haas walked into his room.

The man smiled broadly. "I thought you might be interested in this letter."

Zeke took the letter and stared at it. It was from the railroad. He didn't want to open it. He knew what it said. Placing it on the table in front of him, he thanked Mr. Haas for delivering it to him. "But I already know that I didn't get the land. I had ten days to respond."

"Young man, open the letter." Mr. Haas pulled out the chair opposite him and sat.

Zeke put his fork down and lifted the letter. He pressed his lips together hoping to stave off the negative emotions washing through his system from reaching his face. Taking the knife by his plate, he slipped it into the fold and slit the envelope open.

His eyes scanned the page and then he looked at Mr. Haas. "I don't understand."

Mr. Haas smiled. "I sent a letter to Joseph Coleman and asked him about the land. He told me it was an excellent deal. The front piece of that land comes right to the town. The rest is excellent grazing with a small stream that comes from a spring. I took the liberty of sending the paperwork off for you."

"But…" He closed his eyes and prayed that the tears that were filling them wouldn't spill.

"Zeke, you'd make a lousy poker player. A simple thank you will suffice."

Zeke opened his eyes but his emotions were winning this battle. He pressed his forefinger and thumb to his eyes. "Thank you, sir. If I could choose a father, I would pick you."

Mr. Haas stood and clamped his hand on Zeke's shoulder. "Get well. Everyone misses you, even Phyllis and Suzanne. They keep asking me why you went away. And Shep sits waiting for you to step off the train. I swear that dog cries every time a train comes through." Mr. Haas started to walk out the door and then turned. "You owe me four hundred dollars for the land. You're a good man, Zeke."

Zeke buried his face into his hands. When he pulled himself back together, he reread the papers. The money he'd put down on the other property was transferred to this one and Mr. Haas paid the difference. Zeke knew he had the money to repay his boss. Now he was more anxious than ever to see the property.

He grabbed his crutches and stood. *Will I ever walk again?* He looked at his toes that were purplish-pink and swollen. Attempting to put his foot to the floor sent a burst of pain shooting up his leg. He found the writing paper, the ink and the pen. He needed to write to Mattie and tell her what happened.

Three times he tried to write, and each time, he crumpled the paper and tossed it into the fireplace. *What do I write? I have my land, but I might be too crippled to work it?*

Matilda took the book she was reading into the schoolyard

and sat on the bench under the tree. The air was crispy and a few brown leaves fluttered across the green grass. The trees around her were adorned in reds, yellows, and oranges. She couldn't remember a prettier day in ages. But something inside of her kept poking at her heart, reminding her that Zeke hadn't written to her in ages. Was he all right? Had something happened to him?

She reached in her pocket and withdrew his last letter dated in August. He had applied to the railroad for land in Creed's Crossing. That was more than six weeks ago.

She pocketed his letter and went back to reading. Some books were easy to read and others took more time. Some she enjoyed and some she didn't, but she was almost through the long list of books Mr. Geiger had given her. She wanted to take that exam and get on with her life.

But today, she couldn't concentrate. Every afternoon, she'd help in the Hillerman kitchen, learning to cook a variety of foods. She loved to bake. Her rolls and breads gave her the greatest sense of accomplishment. She wanted to learn more and to do more. A simple visit to the bakery in Germantown told her there were all sorts of wonderful treats to learn. That morning she had slipped a few coins in her pocket and intended to see if she could find a few cookbooks for sale before returning to the Hillerman house.

When school ended for the day, Miriam wanted to come with her, but Priscilla wanted to go straight home. "Well, I'm going to see if I can buy a cookbook. Tell your mother that I have Miriam with me and we'll be along shortly."

In the dry goods store, Matilda found three cooking books and one that was devoted to baking.

"Matilda," Miriam called from the other side of the shelving, "Look what I found!"

Matilda wandered to the other side that contained patterns for clothing. "Oh, look at this sweater, it would be perfect on Zeke."

"Buy the pattern. Momma will teach you to knit." Miriam pulled another pattern. "And this one, too. A scarf is a good way to start." She reached into several cups and found four needles. "You'll need these."

"What about the yarn to make it?"

Miriam rolled her eyes. "Why do you think we have sheep?"

"What do they have to do with it?"

"You'll see." Miriam giggled. "You must have been living in the middle of nowhere."

As Matilda went to pay for her items, she spotted a basket with a hinged lid. It reminded her of the baskets that Gray Fox's mother would make, but this one had a fancy lid. "Do you have beads?"

The friendly woman behind the counter smiled. "What sort of beads?"

"Tiny ones." Matilda pinched both forefingers and thumbs together. "The size of seeds."

The woman opened a large drawer. "We sell them by the ounce."

Matilda took the envelope the woman offered her. The colors were mixed and she hesitated. She took two scoops, knowing she had more than enough. "How much is this?"

The woman weighed them on a small scale. "Seven ounces."

"I also need heavy thread."

The woman produced a small spool.

Matilda counted her coins and then nodded. "I believe I have enough."

Her purchases left her with three pennies, and they decided to stop at the bakery for a cookie they could share.

When they arrived at the house, Matilda ran upstairs and changed into a plain dress that didn't require a corset. Now she could breathe. She washed her face and hands before returning to the kitchen.

Mrs. Hillerman suggested Matilda grate the potatoes for potato pancakes. "And we'll have corn to go with it."

"Do you mind if I make something else?" She opened the pantry cupboard and looked for the cornmeal. In this house, flour was the staple, not cornmeal. Finding only finely ground corn that was labeled cornstarch and some creamy canned corn, she thought about it. Knowing that the powdery corn would save her the time of grinding the cornmeal to a finer consistency. Willing to try, it only took her a few minutes to mix all the ingredients together. Making it with sweet butter would be extra tasty. Never in her life had she seen a pantry that rivaled what she saw in the company store. Every meal in the Hillerman house was wonderful. The corn pudding would be the perfect accompaniment with the spicy scrapple.

"I bought two patterns today at the dry goods store and knitting needles. I was hoping you would show me how to knit. Miriam said I didn't need to buy yarn."

Mrs. Hillerman laughed.

Matilda liked the laugh. It was full, sweet, and reminded her of her mother's laugh.

"My dear, I will teach you to knit, but I must say I've never seen anyone tackle so many new things at the same time. Are you certain you can learn them all?"

"If you teach me to knit, I will teach you to bead."

Everyone loved the corn pudding and deep inside, Matilda could feel the swell of pride that filled her. It was not that she lacked cooking skills, but she had never had many ingredients and no one ever showed her how to make other things. This family ate meals with meat every night, whereas she mostly had beans or a few vegetables with only small amounts of meat because her father couldn't afford more. Now she wondered how he was faring without her. Guilt stabbed at her for leaving him.

After dinner, she showed Mrs. Hillerman her basket. Using a scrap of material, she lined the basket and rolled that material over the top edge of the basket. That edge she intended to cover in beadwork of a common Lakota design. She measured another strip of material and cut it to fit the basket. Holding that strip between her fingers, she began to do her beadwork, stitching and tying as she went.

Priscilla watched over Matilda's shoulder and Mrs. Hillerman paid close attention as the simple design began to appear.

"Who taught you to do that? And what sort of design is that?" Mrs. Hillerman asked.

"Gray Fox's mother."

"Gray Fox? Animals can't sew." Priscilla said in a slightly

haughty tone.

"Gray Fox is my friend. We discovered each other many years ago. He's a Lakota Sioux Indian. I don't care what others think about the Sioux Indians, they have always been nice to me. His mother… his family has always been kind to me. I've even met the chief and many members of the tribe. I taught Gray Fox English and he taught me Sioux. But Gray Fox never learned our written language. I kept telling him he needed to learn. Now, I can't write to him and tell him about my life here in Germantown."

"Can't you write to his agent?" Mrs. Hillerman asked.

"Not exactly. His tribe isn't living on the reservation. We've broken so many treaties with the Sioux that many of the tribes ignore our government. Then someone decides to send the Army after them. Gray Fox's tribe is small and they stay mostly on what is considered hunting grounds. They don't trust us so they stay away from us."

Priscilla crossed her arms over her chest. "But you said you are friends with them. How can that be?"

Matilda lifted one shoulder and let it drop. "Gray Fox and I are childhood friends. Children often follow their fathers when they hunt and they practice with their spears. I guess you could say I discovered Gray Fox. I didn't even know he was an Indian back then. I only knew I had found a playmate. I was lonely and we became friends. Because of that, his family accepted me. I wasn't scared of them. To me, they were his family." She counted her stitches and began to repeat what she had beaded.

"His mother taught me how to make cornbread… and how to skin a rabbit and how to preserve the fur. But they would only be near me in the spring and in the fall. They would move further north and west in the summer, and then they went into a southern valley during the winter."

"It sounds like a tall tale to me." Priscilla huffed.

"Think whatever you want. It was my life."

"Does that pattern have any special significance?" Miriam asked.

"Maybe." Matilda looked at what she was doing. "The white and yellow are on top so I guess that's the moon and the sun, or maybe the white is heaven. This is probably the big bird. I'd say eagle, but it might mean more to them. This could be mountains or water. They never taught me those things. To me, it's a pattern that I often see."

"Momma!"

"Priscilla, calm down. Your brother has written many times about the Indians out there, and I remember him saying when he met Matilda, she was with a young male Indian."

Matilda could feel her stomach twisting into a tight knot. "Did he tell you what all happened that day?"

Mrs. Hillerman cocked her head for a moment. "Nothing much other than he thought you were in trouble, and he found out later that the Indian was your friend."

Matilda giggled. "It must have looked very strange to Zeke. Gray Fox used to like to sneak up on me and try to scare me. It rarely worked. That day I'd seen the hunting party off in the distance. I knew they were in the area. As I said, I have no fear of them. They are my friends." She held out the envelope to Mrs. Hillerman. "Why don't you use the colors I'm not using, and try it. The trick is to keep everything very even and keep it secure. Otherwise, if the thread breaks, the whole thing would come apart. By knotting as I go, it doesn't."

Mrs. Hillerman picked up a scrap of material and seemed to examine it. "Any pattern?"

Matilda nodded and then pointed to the woman's skirt. "You could cover the leaves or the flowers in beads. For the Indians, beads are stones or seeds, not glass like these. These would be very precious to them. They create intricate designs and decorate special clothing with them or create... I guess you would call it jewelry with them." Matilda watched Mrs. Hillerman. "Okay, now knot it and keep going. That's right. Loop and add another bead."

Miriam picked up a scrap and attempted to do it, but soon gave up. "That's too small for me. Besides I hate sewing."

"My mother used to sew and she told me that keeping the stitches tiny and even was important. Then Miz Goode, a lady where I lived, showed me some more."

"Didn't anyone think it was strange for a boy to be learning all skills that are normally for women?" Mrs. Hillerman asked without looking up from her beading.

"Everyone thought I was a good boy for looking out for my father and brother. But sometimes some of the men would look at me with a strange look on their faces. My father would tell me to stay far away from them."

"That's scary." Miriam said.

Matilda shrugged. "There were few women at the mining camp when we arrived there and passing me off as a boy… I hated it. But I realize it kept me safe."

Mrs. Hillerman smiled. "You don't have to pretend to be a boy here."

"I love wearing Miriam's dresses, but I think a few things are getting tight, or I'm getting fat." Matilda returned Mrs. Hillerman's smile.

"You were much too thin when you arrived. You've put on a few pounds and you look much healthier. We'll have to make you some more clothes. You are still much smaller than Miriam."

"Will you teach me to sew a whole dress?"

Priscilla stood. "Oh, Momma, she's just looking for attention."

Dr. Brockmann came into Zeke's room and handed him a piece of hard candy. "How are you feeling today?"

Zeke looked at the man with a heavy German accent and hair black as night. The color was the opposite of Mattie's. Hers was like the sun, so coppery and pretty, as if shot with golden threads.

"I'm feeling much better, and look." He put his foot on the floor. "I was worried about having more surgery, but whatever you did has made a difference."

"Don't go putting weight on it. I don't want you undoing what I did."

Zeke shook his head. "I can't stay cooped up here like a chicken that you are trying to fatten for Sunday's dinner."

The doctor chuckled. "I thought I'd free you for a few days, but I want you back and I don't want you playing cowboy. But I have an idea that I think you might like."

Zeke stared at the doctor. "What?"

"There's a man by the name of Barrett in town and he's looking to open a store. From what I've heard from Arnold Haas, Creed's Crossing just might be the place for him to do that."

Zeke nodded.

"I was thinking you might be the one to take him there. It will give you a chance to leave here for a few days but still keep you somewhat quiet. I don't want you wrestling steers. Plus you'll be able to look at that property of yours."

"As much as I'd like to take you up on that offer, I don't even have a coat with me."

"I asked Mr. Haas to send some things over for you. The family's cook fixed you up with a few things. I'm going to give you today to walk around Hanover and see how you are tonight. If all is well, you'll be allowed to leave tomorrow." Dr. Brockmann chuckled again. "Let me see if I can re-bandage this leg so you can pull your pants over it."

Zeke watched what the man was doing and how he wrapped the leg. "Why do I get the feeling that you are doing this so that I don't forget and try to use the leg?"

The doctor feigned surprise. "Did you go to medical school and somehow fail to tell me that?"

"No, sir."

Dr. Brockmann laughed heartily. "I don't want you using this leg. It's that simple. It's not totally healed yet. You keep asking if you're going to be crippled, and I'm trying very hard to prevent that. Don't undo what I've done. I don't want any pressure on this leg or foot."

After a little more conversation, the doctor released Zeke to wander the town. Breathing in fresh air and being able to walk around, even on crutches, was exhilarating. But it was more than he had done in weeks, and very quickly he discovered he was worn out. He propped himself against the wooden rail in front of the one store and watched whatever traffic there was in the small town. He recognized a few people and tipped his hat to a few of the ladies. One pretty young woman openly flirted with him until he could feel the heat headed for his cheeks.

He looked at his hands. The calluses had peeled from them, leaving his hands soft and white. Then he noticed someone had polished his boots. His memory of that fateful day had slipped from him and he tried to recall what had happened. He replayed what he remembered of the whole incident. Maybe the ordeal was a way of forcing him to look at something that he'd long known. He was not a cattleman.

His dad kept a few dairy cows and sold the male calves off when they reached the age of two or occasionally he'd butcher a steer for the family table. They kept pigs for the family table and sold off most of the young ones to other farmers. But his mom always had lambs. They were gentle creatures, more like pets and their wool became sweaters, socks, scarves, hats, etc.

But the vast majority of the wool was spun and sold. Everyone loved his mom's yarn, especially what she called her baby yarn.

His dad had built a room off the kitchen to hold her dyes and all her yarn. There was a garden for the kitchen and another for making dyes. His oldest sister, Ruth, would spend hours working with their mother to create beautiful yarn colors and keep track of the dye lots. Ruth was so skilled with dyes that she went to work for a company in New York that made rugs.

Zeke recalled his father laughing about how his wife made more money than he did, which was probably true, but it was his dad who kept food on the table and provided for the family.

Zeke leaned forward on his crutches and took off down the street. He needed to build strength and he wasn't going to do that leaning against the rail.

He thought about his land and worried a little about what he'd find. Having bought a pig in a poke, he wanted to see what he bought. How much land was for grazing and how many steers did he dare to raise on it? He watched other men almost lose their ranches over low steer prices, and he'd watched many become instant millionaires. What would he do? His confidence waned. *Can I do it?*

SIX

With effort, Zeke climbed next to the driver of the small coach. "Hello, I'm, Zeke Hillerman."

"Welcome. I'm Bill Barrett. I hear you know your way to Creed's Crossin'."

"I've been there. Bought some land."

"Heard it's in the middle of nowhere and they could use a store." The man slapped at the reins and the horses took off. "I was born and raised in a store. Ain't nothin' I don't know about one."

Zeke listened to the man ramble. "Then why aren't you at that store?"

The man laughed. "Seems my daddy had a passel of boys. I'm the next to the youngest."

"I know about that." Zeke continued to talk and found Bill Barrett to be a nice guy. Surprisingly, they had quite a few things in common.

The trip still seemed to take much longer than Zeke's first trip to Creed's Crossing. They stopped every few hours on Dr. Brockmann's advice and Zeke stretched his good leg for a couple of minutes. They also stopped in various towns along the way and bought meals. But when darkness descended, they took turns sleeping. Zeke was surprised at the stamina Bill possessed as a shopkeeper.

When a small band of Indians crossed their path, Zeke eyed his companion. Mattie had spoken about the local Indians in a good light so many times he had no concern. When Bill reached for a rifle Zeke stopped him.

"They are men... traveling. There's no point in being hostile."

The Indians circled them and forced them to stop.

Zeke nodded at the oldest one. "We're going to Creed's Crossing." The men pulled their horses to a halt, so Zeke continued, hoping he to talk his way out of trouble. "Joseph Coleman said there was good land there."

The men looked at each other and one said, "Car."

They started to ride off and Zeke called, "Wait! Will you help us?"

The one who had spoken turned around.

"What are you doing?" Bill asked.

"Simple, I want a ranch and you want a store. I want my animals to be left alone and you will need to have supplies delivered. We don't need enemies." He looked directly at the young Indian. "How far is Creed's Crossing?"

The man pointed to the sun and then at the east, raising his arm to show the path of the sun and when he indicated the sun setting he pointed down.

Zeke turned to Bill. "Another full day."

Bill shook his head.

Zeke decided to try conversing. "Do you live near here?"

"Live?"

"Tipi, camp?"

The man pointed to a spot in the east.

Zeke pushed onward. "Are you a father?"

The conversation was stunted and awkward, as the man knew only a few English words. But by the time they had parted ways, Zeke knew they were traveling on hunting grounds and from what he could decipher, this tribe refused to stay on the reservation. Zeke also knew that these men weren't really friendly. Was there a trap ahead?

They rode a few more miles and they came across a stagecoach that had broken down. Zeke knew with his broken leg, he wasn't going to be of much help, and Bill couldn't do it alone. But on the horizon were the Indians they had met earlier.

Zeke asked the driver, "What do you have to trade for help?"

"What do you mean?"

"Food, blankets, something."

Zeke shook his head at the driver's ignorance.

"I can pay." The man showed a handful of change.

"I'll find help." Zeke walked away from the stage, whistled, and waved his hands.

The same Indian men came forward, but this time, probably the entire male tribe on horses filled the crest on the horizon.

Zeke met the men. "Can you help to lift the stage so they can put the wheel on?"

The now familiar Indian pointed to his leg.

Zeke walked to a small scrubby bush and removed a twig. "Leg." He snapped the twig. "Our doctor fixed it." He took a blade of grass and tried to straighten out the twig and wrapped it with the blade of grass. "Now it must heal."

The Indian nodded and a child screamed.

Zeke walked up to the coach. "Everyone out. No man can lift this thing while you are all in it."

The child continued to scream and Zeke noticed the mother was just as frightened. Propping himself with one crutch he reached into the coach and took the screaming child in his free arm. "Why are you doing all this yelling?"

The child wiggled and slithered in his arm.

"Stop it! Tell me what is wrong."

The child pointed to the Indian.

"Him? He is my friend." He pointed to another Indian. "He has a little girl your age. I bet you'd like a friend to play with you. She has dark hair like her daddy's."

The child looked at the man standing near her. "Can I play with her now?"

Zeke answered. "She's home with her mommy."

With one heave, the Indians lifted the coach enough for the replacement wheel to slide onto the axel. A moment later, the wheel was secured and everyone could return to the stagecoach. The coach's driver offered the Indians several things and finally the one spoke up and asked for money.

The driver acted as though it was a holdup.

Zeke shook his head. "Just give them some money."

The driver produced several dollars and handed them over. The men left happy and Zeke realized that he'd not only made friends but he'd taught some others to treat the Indians like normal men. He and Bill Barrett parted from the stagecoach and continued on their way to Creeds' Crossing.

Darkness descended and Bill turned over the reins. While the man slept, Zeke continued onwards. Just knowing they were getting close gave him a certain feeling of peace, but with it came an excitement. He was a landowner. He sat a little straighter in his seat.

To his left, he heard the thundering of what sounded like a stampede. As it drew closer, he could tell it was a large band of Indians. As they approached, they began to make strange cries, which awaken Bill. Slightly confused, Zeke pulled to a stop. The Indians circled and Zeke waited patiently. One fired a gun into the air and Bill started to reach for the rifles.

"No. Let's see what they want," Zeke warned in a soft tone.

"You make friends with them and this is what we get? We need to kill as many as we can."

"No," Zeke hissed. "They are men like us."

One Indian put a gun to Zeke's side while another touched his wrapped leg.

"It's broke." He put his fists together and then rolled them down to show breakage. "The doctor put them together and wrapped it."

Behind him they pulled Bill from the cart.

"What do you want from us?"

One man came forward. "We want food and money."

Zeke rolled his palms up. "We are almost at our destination. We do not have much left."

Zeke was pleased he had convinced Bill to remove most of his money from his pockets and hide it. Zeke had less than three dollars on him, but he knew Bill had more. Zeke pulled a small pouch from his pocket and emptied the contents into his own hand.

The Indian went to snatch it.

"No. I will share with you. How much do you need?"

Two of the men looked at each other. "All money."

"If you take my money, will you give me food?"

"All."

Zeke knitted his eyebrows. "Trade!"

Bill hissed, "Give it to them."

"How much did they take from you?"

"Over ten dollars."

Zeke could feel his jaw drop as he spun in his seat to see his travel partner on the ground. "You gave them that much?"

"They are going to kill us!"

Zeke felt that rifle being pushed into his ribs. He turned and put his hand on the barrel and lifted it towards the sky. "Stop that! No! You don't do things like that to your brother. I am your brother."

"You white man."

"You red man." He turned to Bill. "Hand me a piece of that bush."

"Are you crazy — it's filled with thorns?"

"I know. That's why I want it."

Bill took forever breaking off a piece and passing it to Zeke.

Zeke then broke it again, reserving a section with a long thorn. "Watch." He stabbed the young Indian's hand and then his own. "See. Blood. We both bleed." He put his hand next to the man's. Then he took the man's hand and let the man feel Zeke's heart beating. Then he took that same hand and pressed it to the Indian's chest. "Heart. Boom. Boom. We both are the same."

The man withdrew and stared at Zeke.

Zeke smiled. "We are men. Are we on your land?"

Something was said, but Zeke didn't understand their words. He assumed the answer was yes.

"I will have land in Creed's Crossing. I will build a ranch."

"Land."

"Yes, land." Then Zeke decided that's not what they wanted to hear when the man's expression turned downward.

The men talked amongst themselves before the one man said, "No land."

"I bought it from the railroad."

Again they talked.

The conversation was sinking into something unpleasant.

He remembered hearing other ranchers complaining about how the Indians knocked down fences. He sat a little straighter in his seat. "When I have a ranch, I want you to come to my land. We will grow vegetables and you can hunt." He smiled broadly. "We will hunt together. Brothers help each other."

Someone shoved Bill back onto the cart and another Indian took the reins from Zeke. Bill trembled and all color had drained from his face. Zeke was doing everything he could to control his own suspicions. The men took them to a high ridge and pointed. Fortunately the sky was clear and littered with millions of diamonds. The moon wasn't quite full but still it was bright enough to allow Zeke to see for miles.

He pointed and said, "Beautiful."

"Nothing to hunt."

"No buffalo?"

"Nothing to hunt."

It was as though someone turned on the lights in Zeke's head. "You need food, meat – to eat, to feed your family."

The Indian nodded. "White man steal from us."

Zeke nodded. "I will not steal from you. I will help my brothers."

"Why be nice to us? We can kill you."

"I could kill you. What good would that do? We have mothers who would cry, and no progress is made for you or for me. We will be neighbors and I will learn your ways as you learn mine."

"No. You take from us."

"No. We will trade." Zeke motioned behind him. "Bill will build a store where you can buy things you need and he will give you money for things he needs."

"What?" There was a plea in Bill Barrett's voice.

"Yes. You will sell to the Indians and they will bring you things that you can sell." Zeke smiled at the man beside him. "I will need help making my ranch. I can hire you to help me. I've heard it said that ranchers often hire Indians to help."

"What is hire?"

"I pay you to help me. You are my friend." He thought about Mattie. "The woman I will marry grew up playing with a Sioux Indian. She speaks the language."

The man narrowed his eyes. "I am Shoshone."

Zeke had heard plenty about the Shoshone and none of it was good. He ran his fingertips over the nape of his neck, hoping to end the prickling feeling.

Matilda took her exams before school let out for the Christmas holiday. She panicked when she looked at a few of the mathematic problems, when she had to correct a paragraph, and again, when she needed a few historical dates. Now she had to wait.

Pennsylvania was cold. It was a different sort of cold from what she was used to feeling. This cold chilled her to the bones, and even in the house, she constantly wore a heavy sweater. She fought to learn to knit. Her stitches were either too tight or too loose. With effort, she managed to make the scarf but didn't attempt the sweater for Zeke. Never had she failed so miserably at anything in her life. She made a second scarf and it wasn't much better.

"I can't do it." She clenched her teeth together. "What's wrong with me?"

Mrs. Hillerman patted Matilda's hand. "Let's try something different." She rummaged in her box of supplies. "Here."

Matilda took the fat wooden thing. "A crochet hook. I can cut the toes from socks and make new ones. But I've never done more than that. And I've never used one that was so large."

"I will teach you to make lovely things. You still need to keep the loops even."

Matilda often had to drop the yarn from her left hand and gather it back again so that the loops didn't become too tight, but this was easier. Before Matilda retired for the evening, she had over eight inches of a scarf crocheted in a pretty pattern. Each row looked even and her spirits soared. But Matilda excelled at hand sewing. Each stitch was perfect. Even Mrs. Hillerman admitted that she could not sew as nicely as Matilda; all she could do was teach her the stitches for fancy needlework and how to make a quilt.

One cold morning, Matilda bundled up in heavy clothing and went into town. The entire town was decorated for Christmas. Green garland wrapped the lampposts and were topped with big red bows. All the store windows were decorated for Christmas and there were wreaths of all sorts on all the doors. She had never seen anyplace that looked as magical.

In the dry goods store, she bought several yards of wool fabric. She wanted to make a quilt for her and Zeke. Most quilts were made with scraps of material, but she wanted new fabric for her matrimonial bed. She also bought embroidery thread and several patterns.

As soon as she arrived back at the farm, she began to cut perfect squares. When she had enough, she folded the rest and put it in the wardrobe in her room. Then she found a set of hoops that fit the squares and began to figure out what she was going to embroider on which squares. She embellished the patterns with tiny beads.

When the mail came, Mrs. Hillerman called up the stairs, "Matilda, you have a letter."

Matilda flew down the stairs and into the kitchen where she found the letter on the table. She opened it and read it. "He's bought land!"

She continued reading. "Twelve hundred acres. He says that is small."

"That is not a little farm," Mrs. Hillerman said, as she stirred a pot of dye on the stove.

"He says it will be spring before he can go there and begin to build a house for us." Matilda turned to her future mother-in-law. "I do not want to wait that long. He wants everything perfect for me. I do not want to stay here when I am capable of helping him build a house."

"Write to him and tell him that. My son is a reasonable man."

"He said he will put the house by the road that runs through town so that I am close to everything." She read some more and when she turned over the page, he had drawn a primitive sketch of the house. She wrinkled her nose. "It's not much of a house."

Mrs. Hillerman looked over Matilda's shoulder. "That's a very old-fashioned house, similar to the Schweitzer house. That house is lovely on the inside. Will it be made of stone?"

"He doesn't say. I will write and ask."

Mrs. Hillerman shook her head. "My son is terrible. He does not write often enough."

"Yes. I know." Matilda returned to her room. Sitting by the window, she went back to embroidering the square. *I miss you so much, Zeke. I want to feel your lips on mine one more time.* She stitched some more and then stopped. *I might have learned to be a lady, but I can still help you.*

Downstairs she heard the clamoring of the Hillerman family. She put her needlework to one side and went to see what was happening.

Mr. Hillerman had brought a tree into the house. Miriam and Priscilla were so excited that they were clapping their hands together. Mrs. Hillerman was worried that it wasn't full enough. Matilda sat on the steps and watched the commotion, trying to decipher why Mr. Hillerman would bring a tree into the house.

Two hours later, there was something called a Christmas tree in the parlor. The pine tree had been decorated in all sorts of pretty objects that had been stored in a closet under the stairway. And by the following morning, the entire house had been decorated for Christmas. The normal candles were replaced with green ones that were scented with pine. She learned how to make pine roping that seemed to decorate everything.

Mrs. Hillerman put away her dyes and began to make fancy cookies of all sorts and something she called plum pudding. Then she withdrew a large tin lined in parchment paper. The cake inside was wrapped in cheesecloth and she added something she called brandy to the cake. When the scent of alcohol hit Matilda's nose she knew what it was and was surprised to see that it was being poured over a cake.

There was a whole new feeling in the house as Christmas approached. Matilda was grateful that she had made the scarf for Zeke and bought him a heavy sweater. She had put them in the mail before Thanksgiving, wrapped in white paper and tied with a pretty red ribbon. She'd written 'Do not open until Christmas. Love, Mattie.'

At the same time, she had sent her father two warm union suits and a scarf she had made. She wrote Merry Christmas on the package that contained the scarf and sent the union suits unwrapped. She knew how cold it could be and knew he could use them. She had also included two pairs of heavy wool socks. He had no one to mend his old socks. Knowing her father, he was probably doing well without her. He had tried to protect her and all she had done was hate him for it. Every time she thought about her father, a wave of guilt sped through her.

Snowflakes fell as she walked into town. One of the farmers offered to give her a ride, but she turned it down. There was a feeling of peace as she walked along the road and watched the flakes falling. She wanted to buy a few gifts for the family. Priscilla was not her favorite person, but she managed to get along with the young woman.

Window-shopping was fun. She spotted a comb and brush set, and stepped into the shop. A bell clanged over her head as she did. The whole shop was filled with china and other expensive items imported from Germany. There was a vanity set she wanted for Priscilla, knowing that Priscilla had nothing like it. Then Matilda spotted a fine china pastry set. It contained a large teapot, sugar bowl, creamer, three pastry trays of various sizes, and a dozen teacups. The pale green china was decorated in beautiful, pinkish-red roses. It was expensive compared to several other items in the shop, but Matilda had no idea what anything was really worth. She told the woman who worked there that she wanted it. That left Miriam and Esther. After looking around and not see anything that she thought would be the perfect gift for Miriam, she gave up on Miriam's gift.

But the store did have the prettiest little doll for the youngest member of the Hillerman household. Esther was barely eight years old, and she had a doll with a head, hands, and feet made of wood, but this doll was much smaller and made with porcelain. Mrs. Hillerman kept a large box filled with remnants, and Matilda knew she could stitch several outfits for the small doll.

The woman who worked at the china store packaged everything for Matilda. Carrying her bags, she went to find something for Miriam, Joshua, and for Mr. Hillerman. In the haberdashery, she found Mr. Hillerman a warm, soft shirt and one for Josh. But that still left Miriam. Christmas was getting close and Matilda needed something special for Zeke's next to the youngest sister. As Matilda passed a store that sold furniture, a chest caught her eye. It was deep and not very big but would hold all sorts of things. She tapped her toes to knock off the snow from her boots, and then stepped inside.

"Hello," an older man greeted her.

"Hello. I was looking at that chest in your window."

"The blanket chest?"

She bit at her lower lip. "I was thinking about something a girl could store things for when she married."

"You might like this hope chest." He led her to another spot in the store. "This would hold everything you might want."

Heat flowed to her cheeks and she touched her chest. "It's not for me. I was thinking about a Christmas gift for young woman."

She walked between the various chests and stopped. "This one. But I can't carry it home."

"I can deliver it."

She held up a hand. "I need it for Christmas morning. I will ask Mr. Hillerman if he will pick it up and hide it until Christmas."

She lifted the lid of the deep chest. It was made of cedar and smelled delicious. The outside was carved in flowers. It was perfect for Miriam and suited her personality. The very bottom was a drawer that could hold small items. Matilda wanted to add the first item to it; a teapot she saw at the dry goods store.

She paid for the hope chest and scurried to the dry goods store. The teapot was plain except for the lid, which had a bee. As much as Miriam loved honey in her tea, it was perfect and not at all expensive.

Thrilled with her purchases, she started to walk home. The swirling snow that hid her view of the road was accumulating and each step sent her foot deep into the soft white blanket. Her pretty gray wool coat wasn't the same as the leather one she'd worn in Wyoming that was fur on the inside. She shivered.

Gradually appearing out of the white haze came a horse and a cart. "Matilda?"

"Here!" She raised her hand and waved. "Mr. Hillerman. I'm so happy to see you."

"What are you doing out in this storm?"

She told him about the chest.

Mr. Hillerman shook his head. "This snow could keep everyone home for weeks. Let's get it now."

He slapped the reins and went into town. Mr. Schuller wrapped the chest in several layers of paper and then covered it with an old quilt. "Bring my quilt back! I keep it for times like these."

Soon she and Mr. Hillerman were on their way back to the house. She touched Mr. Hillerman's hand. "I'm so sorry. I had no idea it was going to snow this much. I wanted to do some Christmas shopping, and it was so pretty when I left."

"You need to learn to look at the clouds. These clouds were too low and too thick for a dusting of snow."

"I'm truly sorry."

He put his hand on her knee. "I'm certain you are. And you've learned much since you've been with us. And this is one more thing."

They rode in silence for a ways and then she said, "My family was poor. I never had much. We never had a Christmas tree or anything. I don't think my father ever thought about it."

"You didn't need to buy gifts for any of us."

"But I wanted to do it."

"That chest was expensive."

"Will you hide it until Christmas morning? I want to surprise Miriam with it."

"And where will I hide it? It's large and heavy. You can help me take it into the house when we arrive."

"But it's not Christmas."

"And Miriam is not a child."

Feeling chastised, she kept her words to herself the rest of the way home. When they reached the house, she helped Mr. Hillerman take the chest into the house, not only into the house, but also up to Miriam's room.

"Why is it going into my room?" Miriam had followed Matilda up the stairs.

"Because it's your Christmas gift." Matilda gasped for a breath. She wasn't used to doing much physical work since coming to the Hillerman house and doing everything in a long skirt made the job twice as difficult.

When it was in Miriam's room, Matilda stood and put her hands on her lower back. "I need to spend some time chopping firewood. I think my muscles are becoming soft with disuse."

Mr. Hillerman looked at her with total surprise. "That is a man's job."

She shrugged. "I used to do it. It was my job."

Matilda pulled her coat off and then sat on the floor to remove her wet boots.

Priscilla stood in the doorway. "Some lady. You act more like a child."

Matilda wanted to stick her tongue out, but she didn't dare. That *would* be childish. Priscilla always acted as though anything beyond her embroidery might dirty her fingers. Priscilla even complained if she was asked to peel potatoes. The most Matilda could do was hold her tongue. "Well, Miriam, pull the paper off of it. Merry Christmas from me."

"From you?" Miriam unwrapped the chest from the heavy paper that protected it. "It's beautiful. Thank you." She ran her fingers over it. "Momma, look what she gave me."

"I never…" Mrs. Hillerman looked directly at Matilda. "That's a very expensive gift."

Matilda was standing on her feet, holding her wet boots. "I wanted something special for her. Didn't you say that gifts were to come from the heart?"

Mrs. Hillerman nodded. "Yes, but it's the thought, not the price tag."

"Well, it's the thought, because the money doesn't mean anything to me." She turned her gaze from Mrs. Hillerman to Miriam. "Miriam, enjoy your chest."

After leaving Miriam and Esther's room, Matilda went to the one she shared with Priscilla. There, Matilda changed into a plain wool dress that she could wear around the house and put dry wool socks on her feet. She smiled as she pulled on a comfortable pair of slippers and then made her way to the kitchen to help with the evening meal.

She met Mr. Hillerman who was carrying several packages. "You left these in the cart."

"Thank you, sir. And thank you for helping with the chest and bringing me home."

"You are welcome but pay attention to the weather next time."

He left and didn't return until the supper was served. By then everyone was seated around the large table. Mrs. Hillerman had made corned beef, and Mr. Hillerman cut a large slice for everyone present.

The meat was tender and tasty. Matilda was glad she had mashed the potatoes and then whipped them with milk and butter. It was hard work, but the fluffy texture was perfect.

After dinner, everyone moved into the parlor. Mrs. Hillerman was busy knitting and Matilda worked on her squares. Miriam and her sister also did some needlework. Esther played with her doll. Matilda finished the last small square and began to work on the larger center one. Using her thread and a few straight pins, she found the exact center and marked the pattern on the wool. It would be a tree made of names and she couldn't wait until the day would come that she could add the names of the children that she would have with Zeke. Until then, those branches would remain empty. She had bought a brushed cotton for the back and she intended to quilt the front and the back together with a series of patterned stitches that Gray Fox's mother had taught her. It would look like animal tracks but Matilda knew it would be perfect with the flowers and tree designs. Weeks of work had gone into it and Mrs. Hillerman was going to let Matilda stuff it with wool batting.

When she reached a point of being too tired to do more, she packed everything up and excused herself. She barely could stay awake long enough to wash her face and brush her teeth. She put her things away and climbed into bed.

She never heard another sound until she opened her eyes to a new day. Snow was packed against the windows making the bedroom darker than usual. She slipped into the wool dress she had worn last night and quietly made her way down the stairs to the kitchen. No one was there, so she started the fire in the stove, and then mixed up a batch of cornbread. Leaving the cornbread on the wooden counter next to the china cabinet, Matilda grabbed her coat and went to see if she could find any eggs under the family's chickens.

She stepped into the henhouse and the girls barely squawked. Under each hen, she felt for eggs and filled her coat pockets with what she could find. Seven eggs would have to be enough. In her mind, she envisioned the eggs on top of the cornbread, and on top of those would be fried pieces of bacon. She could almost taste it. If she could slice the slab of bacon so it was paper thin, Mrs. Hillerman wouldn't mind her taking the meat. This family fed her more meat in a month than she'd had in her entire life and she was no longer a scrawny thing. Even her breasts had filled out. She liked the way she looked.

As she opened the back door, she could smell cornbread burning. *What?*

Her pan of cornbread batter was upside down on the stove, and everywhere it had run, it was now burning into place. She grabbed a towel and lifted the pan. There was nothing to do but use a spatula and start scraping. She opened the back door hoping that the smell would go outside.

Mrs. Hillerman entered the kitchen. "What happened? I thought the house was about to burn to the ground."

Matilda wanted to cry or scream or perform some violent act. She was certain she knew who was behind it, but she didn't understand why. Instead she calmly answered Mrs. Hillerman. "I have no idea. I left the pan over there, and went to the henhouse for eggs. I wanted to surprise everyone.'

"You've managed to do that. I'll fix my husband a slab of corned beef between some slices of bread. He doesn't have time to wait for us."

Miriam joined them. "What happened?" She waved some towels as though she could chase the smell out of the house. "Was that cornbread? I love your cornbread."

Matilda nodded. "I mixed up the batch and left it over there before I went to the henhouse. I wanted to surprise everyone with breakfast. Instead I walked into this mess."

The batter had slid into the seams of the cast iron stove. It was under the burners, in the oven, and on the firebox. The whole place smelled of burnt corn. Twice she burned her arm and several times she burned her fingers, but when she burned her arm for the third time, she yelped. Her skin didn't look raw - it looked black.

Mrs. Hillerman dragged Matilda to the sink and poured

cold water on her arm. Then after filling a large kettle, Mrs. Hillerman told Matilda to put her arm in the water and not to take it out. Mrs. Hillerman made a compress with herbs and wrapped Matilda's arm. Then had her sit at the table.

Silent tears slipped down Matilda's cheeks with the excruciating pain. Barely aware of anything other than her arm, she knew Mr. Hillerman was eating his breakfast and Mrs. Hillerman was cleaning the stove. *Why Priscilla? I've done nothing to you.*

It was late afternoon when Matilda thought she could handle a small cup of tea. Her arm had been wrapped in towels and then packed in snow. The cold had provided the first real relief that she had. But then her fingers looked bluish, Mrs. Hillerman took her arm out of the snow. Matilda could feel her body shaking with a fever. Mrs. Hillerman gave her aspirin and sent her to bed.

She awakened in a sweat. Her arm immobilized. No matter how she wiggled in the bed, it seemed as though she were in a puddle. She remembered someone wrapping and then later unwrapping her arm. She remembered being given sips of tea and more aspirin. But time was blurred, and she didn't like the feeling of being lost between dreams and reality. Mrs. Hillerman came in to the room carrying a big kettle. "You're awake and the worst should be over."

"Oh. I'm soaked."

"Yes, because your fever has broken." She poured water from a big kettle into a pitcher. Then helped Matilda stand. "Lean here and I will bathe you. You're as weak as a newborn kitten."

Matilda couldn't remember her mother bathing her, making the gentle touch of Mrs. Hillerman beyond comprehension. "If I were with my father I would have wrapped the blanket around me and gone to the stream to do this."

"My dear child, I can't believe you wouldn't die of exposure."

"Only if you stay out too long. It's amazing how fast you can wash when it's cold."

Mrs. Hillerman wrapped Matilda up in a sheet, washed her hair, and then helped her dress in a clean nightgown and robe.

"There, dear child, now you can sit near the fire while your hair dries and then have dinner with us. I'm certain you must be starving."

"I am." She leaned against the post of the bed. "I feel as though I've slept for days."

"You have."

"Did I miss Christmas?"

"No, but it is Christmas Eve and everyone is coming over tonight to see the tree."

"Oh, please. I don't want to meet the family dressed like this."

"Nonsense. They all know what has happened. Remember, this is family and family understands." Mrs. Hillerman smiled. "Would you like me to bring your needlework downstairs to keep you busy while I do some cooking?"

Matilda moved her fingers and her arm. "I'd like to try. The quilt I was stitching is in the lower drawer of the wardrobe."

Mrs. Hillerman opened the drawer and then turned back to Matilda. "Maybe that's not such a good idea. I think it's best if you stay quiet for the time being. I forgot it's your right arm that was burnt."

"Well, then, lift the squares. If you put them in my basket, I'll decide which ones I want to put next to each other."

"I'm sorry but your quilt is ruined. Someone has cut the squares into triangles."

"My quilt?"

SEVEN

Zeke made certain the cattle were fed before washing up for Christmas Eve dinner with the Haases. Twice he'd been in the kitchen and the aroma was making him salivate. He put on a clean shirt and pants, and then ran a cloth over his good boots to be certain they looked their best. He tied his bolo around his neck and flattened his collar. Dinner wasn't formal, but he still wanted to look good. He had a sack of marbles for Phyllis, and from a scrap of lumber, he'd whittled a handful of animals and painted them for Suzanne. It seemed the little girls had everything a child could want. He couldn't afford much, but he was certain they'd have a good time playing and sharing their gifts from him.

He'd taken some of his money and bought a music box for Mattie. Then he sent it to his mother to hold until Christmas.

He knew she would wrap it and hide it under the tree. The thought of being there, and watching Mattie open her gifts stirred his love for her. He wanted her – wanted Christmas in his own house with Mattie by his side. He wanted Mattie in his bed and to feel her petite body against his. *I must not think about that or I'll embarrass myself.*

The aroma of pies hit him as he walked through the back door of the Haas house. Cook shooed him to the parlor where a large tree took up a good portion of the room. He tucked his gifts under the tree and greeted Mrs. Haas. The girls came down the stairs like a herd of wild beasts. They hurled themselves at Zeke, and in spite of his bracing for them, they still almost knocked him off his feet as they hugged his waist.

"Do you have gifts for us?"

He patted the heads of the sweet girls who were dressed alike in plaid dresses of green and red. "Would I forget gifts for my favorite little girls?"

They giggled and squirmed away to see what they could find under the tree.

In a few more minutes, Clay and Mr. Haas joined them. The festivities at the Haas house weren't much different from the ones at Zeke's parents'. It only made Zeke a little more homesick. *Next year, I'll have Mattie.*

After all the pleasantries were exchanged, they were ushered into the dining room. Beautiful beeswax candles glowed and cast light on the fancy Christmas china and the polished silver. Zeke took his place on the far side of the table and Suzanne quickly sat beside him with her big smile. The Haas girls reminded him of his own little sisters, Priscilla and Miriam. Miriam was shier, more like Phyllis in personality, and Priscilla was the happy one, who always smiled and seemed to love life. She was his little shadow. She'd follow him anywhere.

The dinner was Bockwurst, hot potato salad, and a type of fruited bread called Stollen. There was plenty of beer to go with it. Before coming here, he'd never had such a beer. The dark beer the Haases drank was completely different from the golden beers he had tasted.

Then Cook served pie. When he was certain he couldn't eat another bite, there were cookies of all sorts that had been decorated for the occasion and something called marzipan that was made to look like miniature fruit.

When everyone was done, the men retired to Mr. Haas' office. There Mr. Haas gave each of them a cigar to smoke. Zeke didn't mind the scent, but trying to smoke it took some effort. If he breathed in the smoke, he'd choke. Mimicking the way Mr. Haas held one, Zeke attempted to make himself look refined. He took a few more puffs and gave up. He knew Clay would finish the cigar for him.

Mr. Haas suggested they light the candles on the tree. The children made little excited noises as the men lit each candle. And when they were done, everyone admired the beautiful tree. Christmas songs were sung and Cook even played the piano. Then Mr. Haas opened the Bible and read the part about the birth of Jesus. Then with great care and using candlesnuffers, the candles on the tree were extinguished. Mrs. Haas allowed the girls to hang their stockings before chasing them to bed. Zeke leaned down and received a hug and kiss from each of the girls. They were royally spoiled, yet such sweet little creatures. Their genuine affection made him realize how much he missed his family.

When Mrs. Haas returned minus the children, Mr. Haas poured a glass of warmed brandy for everyone and more cookies were served along with several chocolates. The evening lasted well past Zeke's normal bedtime and the alcohol was having an effect on him.

"You're being quiet tonight, Zeke, what is on your mind?"

"Sorry, Mr. Haas, I was only thinking about how next Christmas will be."

The man laughed. "I'll tell you what next Christmas will be, cold and miserable if you don't succeed." The man stood and paced a few times in front of where Zeke sat. "Only you can make certain that doesn't happen. Save a few pennies every chance you have all year long. Your neighbors will judge you on your ability to create a nice Christmas for your family. It doesn't matter if your tree is only this high, but make certain it's lovely. Buy a good bottle of brandy or whiskey to share with visitors and keep a few cigars on hand. Give your wife something special, not just something she needs, but give her something unexpected that will make her feel like a queen. Something she can show off to her friends. And make certain there is plenty of food on the table and enough to share. People will judge you, and you need to appear successful at all times.

That night, Zeke's head hit the pillow and his only thought was of Mattie who was with his family.

Clay woke him and handed him a cup of coffee. "Feeling like you had a bit too much last night?"

Zeke pulled himself up on one elbow. "Will this stop the pain in my head?"

"Not really, but it will help. Pull on your clothes. We have cows to milk and chores to do. They don't know it's Christmas."

Two hours later, the chores were done and Zeke was taking a bath in a tub of lukewarm water. He stepped out and dried off quickly in the cool air before pulling on a warm union suit that he had placed near the small stove. He was certain that union suits were the best invention. He pulled on his good pants and his nicest shirt. Combed through his winter beard and trimmed it in a few places along with his mustache. Anyone who worked outside tended to have a beard. It was the only protection against the bitter cold winds. But he doubted his parents would have approved of his whiskered face. Certain he looked his best, he walked to the Haas house.

Shep was already there in the kitchen. That dog had managed to wiggle his way into Cook's heart and she let him in the house all the time. Now he was sleeping in front of the stove with his head on his crossed paws. He opened one eye in recognition of his owner and his tail swept the floor a few times.

Next to Shep stood Cook making waffles. She called a cheery Happy Christmas, as Zeke walked through her kitchen and headed down the hall towards the parlor. The girls were already playing with their new dolls that St. Nicholas had brought them along with a fancy pram for each doll. The rest of the presents sat unopened. They were not allowed to touch those until they had eaten their breakfast.

Mrs. Haas joined the festivities and was dressed for the day, and Mr. Haas came around the corner with a large smile. "Happy Christmas!"

Zeke wondered if Mattie had opened his gift and if she liked it. He wanted to close his eyes and be back in his childhood home with Mattie at his side. Instead, he smiled at his boss and the boss' family. "It's a beautiful day, and those big clouds mean we have snow coming."

Mr. Haas walked to a window. "I believe you are right. Those puffballs tend to grow and thicken until they dump water or snow on us. But for now, they are beautiful. We do have the most beautiful skies out here."

Cook came around the corner. "Who is ready for breakfast?"

After the meal, everyone opened gifts including Zeke. Mr. Haas had given Zeke a pen and ink set. It was fancy and he also was given a beautiful stack of paper and matching envelopes. He envisioned the day when he would have his own office in his house much like the office that Mr. Haas had.

Cook and Clay had given him two pairs of warm socks that Cook had knitted from Merino wool. He loved the feel of those socks and he loved those sheep. They had received a shipment of quite a few heads and Mr. Haas had kept a few for himself. The color of his socks was the natural color of the animals outside. Cook was always using their wool for something.

He liked dealing with sheep. They were by far more intelligent than cattle and they required less care in so many ways, except for shearing.

Clay had grown up on a sheep farm and knew quite a bit about them. Zeke realized that with his mom spinning wool, he, too, had gained a great deal of knowledge about the wool. He wanted to talk to Mr. Haas, but Christmas was not the day to do it. Cattle prices had fallen and several other ranches were raising sheep. *That might be the key to my success as a rancher.*

After a dinner of goose, cabbage, roasted potatoes, more fruited bread and plenty of cookies, Zeke decided he couldn't eat another bite. He excused himself from the festivities and went to his room. There he penned a letter to Mattie and also to his sister Ruth.

Ruth was his oldest sibling and had married a man who worked in the textile industry in New York. The number of years between Zeke and his sister had separated them, yet Ruth had always been kind to him as though he were one of her dolls. This was one time he needed that sisterly advice.

The following morning he was back to work, but instead of being outside, Mr. Haas had Zeke working inside doing the books and acting like an agent. It was a compromise to keep Zeke working after he'd hurt his leg.

The leg had healed, but it had left him with a slight limp that became more pronounced when Zeke was tired. He refused to tell Mattie about it. Deep inside it hurt to think that he was less than perfect, and by some standards, he was crippled.

But doing the books for Mr. Haas had been an amazing experience. Zeke discovered he was actually very good at it, and he enjoyed it. He had the ability to see the big picture while keeping track of all the small things.

Mr. Haas walked into his office with two cups of coffee. "Zeke, have you ever considered being a bookkeeper instead of a rancher? There are plenty of men who know how to take care of cattle, but they have no clue how to keep books. People pay plenty to have someone keep track for them."

"Please tell me more. I'm trying to make some decisions."

"I'll tell you more later. Have you looked outside?"

"No, sir." Zeke looked out the window at the snow falling and sucked in a breath. "I think I'm going to have to help Clay."

Matilda stared at Mrs. Hillerman. "My quilt is ruined?" She crossed the room and looked at the pile of fabric in the drawer. "I'm not going to let that much fabric go to waste. I will make a… I don't remember what they are called… a silly quilt?"

"A crazy quilt."

"No one is going to ruin my quilt. They may have changed it but that is all they have done. Bring it downstairs for me."

Zeke's two uncles came for a few minutes with their families, and then left. They would return tomorrow for the big dinner. Matilda stayed in the background and tried to avoid contact with the family. Having been ill, she managed to pull it off.

No one expected her to do anything. Except when the whole family arrived, Matilda passed around the center square of her quilt and a pencil. "Will everyone please write your name in an open area and then cut out your name?

Mrs. Hillerman smiled as she wrote her name. "But you are missing a few people. You are missing Zeke, our two oldest daughters, and their husbands."

"Will you add their names for me?"

Christmas Eve dinner was a beef crown roast and she wished she had been in the kitchen to see it being prepared. Never had she had such tender meat. Mrs. Hillerman served the roast with something she called Yorkshire pudding. Matilda knew she wanted to learn to make everything she had tasted. She also understood why Zeke had sent her to his family. She had so much to learn and she was trying hard to learn as much as she could.

Christmas morning was filled with surprises, which included a gift from Zeke. She opened the little wooden box and it played music. Then it quit playing and she couldn't figure out how to make it play again until she turned it over and saw a little handle. She turned the handle a few times and it began to play.

Miriam shimmed next to her and craned her neck to see the box. "It's beautiful."

"I know. I've never owned such a wonderful thing." Then Matilda looked up in time to see Mrs. Hillerman open her present.

The woman's eyes grew round and her mouth fell open as she reached into the box and withdrew the fancy rose-covered, green platter. Tears began to fall down the woman's cheeks as she unwrapped each teacup.

Matilda couldn't understand what she had done that was so wrong. She stood, went into the kitchen, pulled on her coat, and stepped out of the house and into the snow. The air was crispy, and it felt good. She cupped some snow in her hands and washed her face with it.

"What are you doing, my dear child?"

"Washing my face. It feels wonderful." She looked at Mrs. Hillerman. "I'm sorry to make you cry. I thought you'd like it for when your friends visit."

"My tears were from joy, not sadness. I saw that set when it first came into the store. I thought how beautiful it was and how someone would be lucky to have such fine china. I never dreamed that person would be me." Tears once again began to spill down her cheeks.

"Here." Matilda scooped up some snow. "Wash you face in the snow. It takes away the tears."

A few moments later, they were back inside with the family. Matilda pointed to a small box. "Miriam, I believe that one is for you."

Miriam crawled under the tree to reach the box. "But you already bought me that beautiful hope chest."

"Well now you will have something to go in it."

Miriam opened her gift to find a fat teapot that was large enough for a family or for a handful of friends to share some tea. "Oh, thank you! It's perfect! I love it."

Mr. Hillerman's gift was in two parts. One was a wool cowl that Matilda had crocheted. It would keep him warm on cold mornings. And the other was his shirt.

Josh seemed happy with his shirt and with a small folding knife that she had bought him. She knew she'd be teaching him how to throw a knife. It was a skill that she never questioned.

Priscilla hung back and kept finding ways to leave the room until her mother called her and told her to sit. There was still a package under the tree for her.

Miriam handed her sister the package. "I can't wait to see what she's given you."

Priscilla opened the package and saw the vanity set. She burst into tears and ran from the parlor.

Miriam looked at her mother and then at Matilda, "What's wrong with Priscilla."

"I have no idea," Matilda said.

Mrs. Hillerman picked up the box that Priscilla had left behind. "What a lovely set. It matches her room." She looked at Matilda and then over her shoulder as though she were checking to see if someone were there. "Miriam, I need you to straighten the parlor while I talk to Matilda in the kitchen."

Matilda followed Mrs. Hillerman into the kitchen. When they arrived, the older woman asked, "What is wrong between you and Priscilla?"

"I have no idea. I don't have a problem."

"You gave her a very nice gift."

"This is the first real Christmas I've ever had. I wanted it to be special. Then everyone has said that we should give gifts from the heart. I tried to find things that were special and just for that person."

"It is Priscilla who ruined your quilt, isn't it?"

"I have no proof."

"Can you think of a reason?"

Matilda filled the kettle with water from the pump at the sink. "I've asked myself a dozen times that same question. I don't have a problem with Priscilla." Then she put the kettle on the stove and checked the wood. "There is no reason for me to treat her any differently. She is the one with the problem. I will not add to her problem. There is no reason for me to put salt to her wound. Furthermore, if the cow quits giving milk, do you ask the chickens why?"

"My dear child, you have a very gracious heart. It is easy to see why my son loves you," Mrs. Hillerman sat at the table and rubbed her forehead. "But you have also given everyone expensive gifts. I know my son does not have that kind of money, and you have said that your family was poor. You have no job or any way to earn money—"

"I didn't steal it. I found some gold in the stream where I lived in Wyoming and traded it for cash on my way here. I wanted to make certain I had my own money and I wasn't a burden."

"My son's future wife is not a burden. And I cannot thank you enough for that beautiful china set."

"Maybe it is because I've never had much, I could only look at things and dream about them. One day when Zeke has built our house, I will be able to fill it with all sorts of lovely things."

"Fill it with love. If you don't, the things will have no meaning."

Oh, Zeke I love you and miss you so much. When can I be with you? I want your lips on mine.

Winter in Wyoming meant snow and strong bitter winds. Zeke was happy he was working inside. Mr. Haas taught Zeke about bookkeeping, and also taught stock and market pricing. It gave him a different perspective on everything. They discussed Zeke's idea of growing sheep for wool. And when Ruth's letter came, Zeke knew sheep farming was the way to go.

Ruth's husband was discouraged in his job. He'd risen in rank to the point that there was no future. It was the owner's family that held the top positions. But Daniel knew the industry, and had been considering starting his own company. Competition was fierce, but he wanted to create a quality product that no one could touch.

Zeke showed Mr. Haas the letter.

"Now you have your outlet. Not too many people have that kind of opportunity. You don't have to go through the open market. You supply the finest wool and they do the rest. You win and they win. But can you supply all that they need?"

Zeke could feel the smile tugging at his cheeks. "How many sheep can you supply?"

"I have no problem brokering."

"I believe I can tell my sister and her husband that we can do this."

That night he wrote to Ruth. He had plans and he knew he could make things happen, but could he build a house fast enough for Mattie?

Matilda spent the winter learning to keep a real house. She wrote everything down and tried to keep it all organized. There was soap for bathing, and one for washing her face, then another for clothes, a different one for floors, and still more for things such as dishes. She learned to make them all and learned the difference in the brands if they were bought.

She learned to cook and learned how to butcher farm animals. But what she loved was learning to sew clothing. Everyone was talking about the Singer Sewing Machine. There were ads for it in magazines so when she saw one in a window of a store in Germantown, she squealed with delight. Two days later, she returned with Mr. Hillerman and they brought the machine home.

Miriam wouldn't even look at it. Her grades were falling and in general she withdrew from most everything.

Matilda had tea waiting for Priscilla and Miriam when they came home from school.

"I can't do it. I want to quit," Miriam professed as she came through the door.

"That's not like you," Mrs. Hillerman said. "Whatever happened to my daughter who loved school? The one who was always happy?"

Priscilla huffed a few times. "She just wants to stay home because Matilda does."

Matilda added the hot water to the tealeaves. "Miriam, can you see? You've been having problems since before Christmas."

"Of course I can see. I'm not blind."

Matilda looked at the tin that contained the leaves. "Here can you read this?"

Miriam took the tin and read, "Assam."

"And what else?"

Miriam shrugged. "There's nothing else."

Mrs. Hillerman took the tin from Matilda. "Miriam, I do believe you need glasses. Why didn't you say something sooner? Tomorrow I'll take you into Philadelphia to the doctor who specializes in eyes."

"May I go with you?" Matilda asked.

"Well, of course, but you're not having problems with your eyes are you?" Mrs. Hillerman had a look of concern on her face.

"No, not at all, but I'd like to see the Wanamaker store."

Concern turned to confusion as Mrs. Hillerman tilted her head slightly and knitted her brow. "I do hope you aren't lacking for anything."

"I have no desire to purchase anything… I've never been in such a store and I want to see it."

"Oh, please, Momma. I want to go there, too," Miriam said.

Matilda gave Mrs. Hillerman the sweetest smile. "I'd also love to see the shops that buy your wool. The last letter Zeke sent mentions raising sheep for their wool. He said there is a market for fine yarn."

"With luck, we can make a day of it. If it takes too long at the doctor's office, we'll make another trip into town." Mrs. Hillerman reached out and patted Matilda's arm. "He wrote to me and asked if you had learned to dye wool."

Matilda laughed. "All recipes are recorded, but you seem to have an intuition about the dyes."

"Practice will teach you. And that is why each dye lot is given a number."

"I think your son assumes that I will know how to do everything when I arrive."

The next day, they sat in the waiting room of the doctor's office until Miriam's name was called. Matilda could do almost anything she tried to do, except sit still for long periods of time. She eventually gave up. "Mrs. Hillerman, I'm going to step outside. At least there is more to see out there."

She wandered down the street looking at all the shops and offices along the way and then made her way back on the opposite side of the street. On the far side of the office, there were houses sprinkled between the shops and she could see where eventually it was all houses.

"Matilda!"

She turned at the sound of her name and saw Miriam running to her. "What is wrong?"

Miriam waved her arms wildly until she had caught up to Matilda. Gasping for breath she stood for a moment until her breathing calmed. But by that time, Matilda saw the glasses on Miriam's face. Set in gold frames, the oval glasses were the least fashionable style.

"They look horrid on me. I know how they look so don't try to do what Momma did and say that I look lovely." Miriam put her hands on her hips and sucked in another deep breath. "But look at the grass. It's…" She made a motion with her fingers. "It's not a solid mat, it's all these little strands. Oh, the whole world looks wonderful! Look at the leaves!"

Matilda took Miriam by the shoulders. "Hush! You are jabbering and making no sense." Matilda smiled at Zeke's sister. "The glasses don't look as terrible as you think. They are far from being stylish, but from what you are saying and the smile on your face, I think you're willing to trade fashion for your sight. Maybe now your stitches will be even."

"Let's go to Wanamaker's. I want to *see* everything!"

A week later, Matilda wrote a letter to Zeke. She tried her best to explain everything she had learned about yarn and about keeping a house. She also told him that she had her own money and that she wanted to help with the finances.

She had been to the ticket office for the railroad and had bought her tickets to Wyoming. She would be taking the Central Pacific and then would come north to Creed's Crossing by stagecoach. The estimated date of arrival would be June 23. *I am only bringing one trunk. I will send for the rest of my things when we are settled into our house. I will meet you in Creed's Crossing. Just thinking about seeing you makes my heart sing.*

Zeke had a handful of letters. He saved Mattie's and opened Ruth's. Daniel was excited about the prospect of opening his own factory and felt as though Wyoming was the best place for it. He reasoned that if the sheep were there, it was easier to ship finished skeins than to ship shorn wool.

Ruth's next letter said Daniel was planning on taking some leave from his job to obtain land in an area with a large enough population to support a factory. The third letter wasn't as cheery. Daniel had been let go from his job so that the boss' nephew could have Daniel's position. Ruth and Daniel were leaving in two weeks for Wyoming.

Zeke had a new pressure forcing him to succeed. He needed to leave the Haas stockyard as soon as he could obtain enough lambs. And the land was empty. He had a house and a barn to build.

"Zeke, your land goes to the town. Don't build a bunch of separate buildings - build one. You can build whatever you need later, but you need a roof over your head as quickly as possible." Mr. Haas sketched a building as he talked. "Here you have a bookkeeping office, a small apartment upstairs, and behind it you have an area that serves as a barn. If you did them separately, you'd have three sets of roofs, this way you have one. That's a savings right there both in terms of time and money." He stabbed the nib of his pen next to the sketch. "The sooner you open your office, the sooner you will begin to make money. You have at least one year before your ranch will pay you a penny."

Zeke nodded.

"Every female wants a grand house. A year from now, you can build one for her. Then you can rent that apartment over the shop, giving you more income."

Everything Mr. Haas said made sense, but the weight on Zeke's shoulders was more than he expected.

"Just remember, those cattle ranchers don't think much of sheep. Or sheepherders."

"Yes, sir. I won't forget."

The following morning, Zeke sent a telegram to his sister. There was no place to stay in Creed's Crossing while he built a house, but Sheridan had a hotel, as did Laramie and Cheyenne. He expected to be bringing a small herd with him to Creed's Crossing on May first. *I need to tell Mattie I'm leaving here sooner than expected.*

In Hanover, he was able to buy a covered wagon. With two horses, a small herd of sheep, and a few building supplies, it was a start. He could order some additional building supplies in Sheridan and have them shipped.

He thought about the library that Mattie so often mentioned and began to draw plans in the evenings. Windows were expensive, but would add light and therefore save on kerosene. But windows facing north would make the building colder. Windows facing… He tossed the plans and started again. After several attempts, he came up with a design that he liked. The apartment was large enough to take the pressure off of him to build a big house. He made a copy of his design knowing he'd need it for the building supplies.

Mr. Haas had some supplies that he wasn't using, such as three partial barrels of nails. Zeke happily accepted the gifts and loaded them into the wagon. Mr. Haas also had several sheets of tin roofing. Zeke estimated the value of everything and knew it was a substantial savings. He was anxious to leave and saddened to leave the Haas stockyard that had become home to him. Cook and Clay had become friends, unlike any Zeke had ever had, and Mr. Haas was often more like a father than a boss. The man had tucked Zeke under a protective wing and taught him more than Zeke ever dreamed.

Zeke knew how to do a profit and loss sheet that could be taken to the bank if he needed a loan. Zeke's dad had taught Zeke to be thrifty and to save money, but Mr. Haas had taught the value of money and the fine art of putting money to work. But all the teaching didn't mean a thing if he failed. That was one scenario that Zeke didn't want to contemplate.

Matilda made plans. Her little book was filled with everything that she thought might be useful. She had a small box filled with seeds - some were vegetables and others were flowers or herbs. After almost ten months with Zeke's family, she had gained a tremendous amount of knowledge. Plus she had her certificate saying she had passed her final exams. Her knowledge of some of the finer points of the history of Penn's Woods was a bit sketchy, and she never was very good at remembering dates, but she had managed to complete the exam. She had barely passed, but she had passed, and that was all that had mattered to her.

She spent a day in the library in Philadelphia making notes on all sorts of things including how everything was cataloged. But she'd also never forgotten the day that Lena had given her the copy of Harper's Bazaar. Lena was done with it, and for Matilda, it was one of the most exciting things she had ever read. She had hidden it in her bed and read every word in it. And when she was done with it she passed it to Miz Della Garfield. Magazines were important to women and if they would donate them to the library, everyone could enjoy them. She envisioned her library bulging at the seams with books and magazines.

Mrs. Hillerman threw a party for Matilda and invited friends and neighbors. Sixteen women packed Mrs. Hillerman's parlor and she served most of them with her pretty set that Matilda had given her. The rest of the women and family members were served with plain china. They all seemed to think that Matilda was brave for going to the frontier.

"Oh, but it's not new to me. I spent the first half of my life in California and the second half of my life in a tiny mining town in the Wyoming territory."

"But you must be careful, there are those horrible savages out there," a neighbor said with great concern in her voice.

"Yes, there are Indians. I had one for a playmate. They are people, much like anyone in this room, except they don't live in fancy houses. If Mrs. Hillerman lived in Wyoming, my Indian friends would be sitting here with us sipping tea and worrying about me moving so far away. They love their children, respect their parents, and love their spouses. They don't go to the grocery store or the dry goods store. The hunt and they make whatever they need." *When will people understand?*

After a reasonable length of time, the women left but each had given Matilda a recipe and several had brought a token gift. Matilda had enjoyed her party and thanked each guest as they left. Mrs. Hillerman had given the guests a little gesture of friendship in the form of fancy cookies. And that night Matilda copied each recipe that was given to her so that Mrs. Hillerman also had a copy. *Maybe the library could use a recipe box. I'm sure there are many more wonderful recipes that women would share.*

It seemed as though she had more things to do in those last few weeks than she'd ever had in her lifetime. She packed only the most necessary things in the one trunk and packed everything else for shipping later.

"What about your sewing machine?" Mrs. Hillerman asked. "Certainly you will want that once you are settled."

Matilda looked at Miriam. "When I'm ready for one, I will buy another. It seems that since Miriam started wearing glasses, she's enjoyed sewing. Consider it my gift to the family for allowing me to stay here."

Miriam's grin was contagious.

Matilda learned to wash and card the wool, but spinning required practice, and she didn't have the time to become skilled at keeping the wool even as she spun. Dying, she enjoyed. There was something satisfying to see the yarn turn colors and to know that she had created the color.

She double-checked to be certain she had every recipe for the table and for the wool. Even Mrs. Hillerman went through her collection and added a few more things to it. Satisfied, Matilda packed them into the trunk that she was taking with her. She had made three simple dresses that she could wear while helping Zeke so that she didn't have to wear pants and she had several pairs of shoes. Mrs. Hillerman made her a beautiful, crocheted, cotton shawl that she could wear in the summer and gave Matilda the instructions so that she could make more if she wanted. And also in the trunk was a white nightgown made of the sheerest fabric that was delicately embroidered and trimmed in lace that Matilda had bought for her wedding night. And for her wedding, she had the palest green dress with a border of pink roses and dark green leaves at the hem and a dark green waist tie that made a bow over the bustle. There were matching green gloves and a lovely little bustle hat in light green trimmed with a darker green ribbon and pink roses.

"I'm going to miss seeing my son marry, but I understand that he can't take the time to come home." Mrs. Hillerman brushed the tears off her cheeks. "But having you here has been a blessing for I've grown to love you as my own daughter."

Matilda turned and hugged Mrs. Hillerman. "Maybe no one can ever replace a mother who has been lost." She smiled at the woman who was trying to withhold her tears. "You have become special to me. Someone I can lean on and trust like a mother, but with the closeness of a dear friend."

"When you first came, I wondered what my son saw in you. Now I know. You aren't afraid to tackle any job. And you have some most unusual skills for a woman."

"You must be talking about my ability with a knife." Matilda laughed. "You should see me with a spear."

"I can imagine. It must be difficult to live in the West."

"You must be strong to survive."

Matilda knew she was going to have a difficult time leaving. Priscilla's jealousy was Priscilla's problem, not Matilda's, and she never understood why the young woman was envious. But Matilda didn't let the cut up quilt squares stop her from finishing it. She pieced things together and made a crazy quilt and that block in the center was cut so that the tree stood alone. Every piece the family had signed, Matilda had carefully embroidered the written names. And to keep it from being too short, she added an edge that resembled a log cabin design. Mrs. Hillerman gave Matilda wool batting for the quilt, and with the wool tacked into place, Matilda did an animal track design over the whole thing. Everyone thought it was beautiful.

When it was completed, she presented it to Mrs. Hillerman. The woman asked for some thread and then proceeded to embroider one more name on the edge. Apparently Zeke had a sibling who had died at the age of two.

It was much too warm in the summer to use such a quilt so it was packed away. But Matilda knew that Mrs. Hillerman was thrilled with the quilt and Priscilla would always know that she had attempted to destroy it. Matilda could hear her brother's words as if he were standing beside her. *Being angry doesn't do anything. Find a way to make them angry. They are the ones who will lose.* Matilda knew it was mean, but it was Priscilla's problem.

Matilda was counting down the days to her departure, to her new life in the Wyoming Territory with Zeke. She was anxious and more than a little nervous, yet the excitement of seeing Zeke sent little trembles through her body.

EIGHT

Zeke arrived in Creed's Crossing with a list of tasks he needed to do quickly. Bill Barrett's mercantile was doing well and Bill's brother Ted had opened a farm supply.

Zeke immediately ordered lumber. Sleeping in the wagon wasn't easy when the temperature often kept water frozen solid. Bill Barrett offered for Zeke to stay over the mercantile with Bill and his wife, and Zeke accepted the generous offer.

"I have less than two weeks to try to at least build something habitable. My sister Ruth and her husband will be coming."

Bill clapped Zeke on the back. "Between now and Sunday, we'll ask everyone to pitch in and help. You'll have something."

Zeke recalled when he was about twelve, a neighbor's house had caught fire and burned to the ground. The following day, the community came together and cleared the charred remains, and the next day there was a house standing. The family still had plenty to do but they could move into the shell and finish it themselves. If the folks here could do something like that for him, he'd be most appreciative.

The farm supply had plenty of barbed wire and Zeke went to work putting up a fence that would hold the lambs that he'd brought with him. Then he marked another area for the two cows and the cheap bull Zeke had brought with him. The old bull was big and docile, yet he still liked the cows. He'd be enough to give a start to the ranch.

"What are you doing with those sheep? This is cattle country." A rancher rode his horse to where Zeke was twisting two peices of barbed wire together.

Zeke knew he'd hear those comments. He smiled broadly. "Pets for yarn. They aren't ordinary sheep. Let me finish putting up some fences so my old dog can have a rest. Then I'll show you the difference."

The man shook his head and rode off. Zeke knew he was going to have a tough time fitting into this community.

Sunday morning, Zeke went to the tiny church in town. It was a short service, but it appeared as though the entire community came and most had picnic baskets. Everyone seemed happy to meet Zeke and inquired about the building.

"Two stories. The first floor will be an accounting office and a library. The upstairs will be our apartment, and behind the building will be a small, attached barn."

Everyone nodded their approval, but the questions

continued about the sheep. Several of the women knew something about yarn and seemed anxious to buy the wool.

"It'll be next year before I can have them sheared again, and my soon-to-be wife has plans for the wool." He figured that might keep him out of trouble.

A few of the men chuckled. "Bringing out a mail order bride?"

He shook his head. "No. Mattie spent her early years in California and then moved to the Wyoming Territory. Last summer, I sent her to my parents home back east so she could finish her schooling."

One of the men raised his eyebrows and walked away.

Zeke figured he'd said the wrong thing, but he didn't know what.

Monday morning, Zeke had his supplies, and as the sun rose in the sky, he had a dozen men ready to build. He tacked his plans to a post and the men went to work. He was glad he'd spent two days creating footings. They built the exterior walls on the ground, and by the end of the day, he had his building, including stairs to the second floor. But when he walked into it, he could tell he'd made a mistake. Everything was larger than he expected.

That night he pondered his situation. *If I put the kitchen and the bathroom downstairs…* The Barrett brothers had sunk a deep well and everyone in town was allowed to hook up to it. But the lines had stopped before reaching his property and they were so deep that he'd have to wait another few weeks until the ground warmed before he could reach the pipe and bring it to his place. It would be work but cheaper and easier than digging a shallow well on his property. *Mattie will be thrilled with running water in the house. Even my parents don't have that.*

Two days later, Ruth and Daniel showed up.

Zeke put his saw down and ran out of the door to greet his oldest sister. Except when he saw her, another ton of weights fell on him. "You are in the family way."

"You're not supposed to notice that, baby brother."

"You never said a word."

She shrugged as she grinned. "If I had, you would have told me not to come."

"True. You have no business being here with... This isn't the big city."

"We couldn't stay in the city or we would have been broke in no time. Rent is expensive." She wandered off and looked at the house. "This is it?"

"It's only partially done. And it's not ready for you."

"Well, we're going to have to manage. Stop worrying."

Daniel looked the place over. "Do you own another saw?"

"No, but the Farm Supply will sell you one."

Ruth and Daniel took over his wagon. But what surprised Zeke was that Daniel could handle a saw. Ruth managed to do the cooking and the other things that they needed, leaving the guys to work almost non-stop on the house.

Daniel nailed the wall to the floor that would separate the office from the library while Zeke held it in place.

"Moving the kitchen downstairs is a good idea. You have plenty of room here."

Daniel built another wall and instead of placing it where Zeke thought it should go, he moved it forward. "Now stand over there while I hold the wall, and tell me what you think."

Zeke did as directed. "You are correct. I still have plenty of office space."

"Then grab the hammer and nails. This wall is heavy."

When they were done, there was a parlor, dining room, kitchen, and bathroom downstairs and a section of what was supposed to have been the barn was taken as a laundry and wool processing area. The upstairs was sectioned off. Instead of two bedrooms there were four large rooms and two small rooms, plus where the stairs came up, there was room for a sitting area.

"Oh, this is wonderful. We won't need to build a separate house. We'll be able to stay here with you and your bride." Ruth smiled at her brother.

Zeke could feel his hackles rising. That was not what he had intended, but he didn't know how to tell his sister that she couldn't stay.

A man from Sheridan came and plastered the walls. The added walls meant more money in plastering, which wasn't cheap. Zeke's money was draining away very quickly. His only option was to explain to Daniel that the money was running out.

"Yes, I understand. That's why we left the city. But I can tell you that we won't be staying here. There's not enough population here for us to even consider to building a mill. My parents have promised to back me on that, but I'm seriously considering Cheyenne or Laramie if they are larger than this place."

Zeke laughed. "Anyplace is larger than Creed's Crossing. Homestead Canyon is nothing more than a mining town and it's bigger than this place." He measured the next piece of molding. "And Mattie thinks she's going to have a big library here? Wait until she sees this place. She'll be lucky if she has three patrons."

Zeke turned and realized that Ruth had to have heard what he said to Daniel.

As Daniel and Zeke finished up for the day, Daniel told Zeke that he wanted to go to Laramie. "I want to leave Ruth here until I'm settled. I don't think it's good for her to be traveling in her condition."

Zeke nodded. He understood, but he wasn't thrilled. Even though Ruth was his sister, he was certain it wasn't proper to have her alone in the house with him. His world was crashing around him and now this new development.

Two days later, Daniel left. Joseph Coleman invited Zeke to his ranch after church and Zeke took the offer, especially when it came with the possibility of supplies and a few pieces of used furniture.

Ruth looked at Zeke. "Go. Don't worry about me. Besides I'm too tired to even care. It's a pretty day and I want to spend some time with the sheep. They do better when they are used to humans touching them."

Zeke hitched the wagon and headed out to the Coleman ranch.

Mattie stared out the stagecoach window and watched the landscape. It was different from Homestead Canyon, similar but different. Everything appeared to be greener for this time of year. The grass was taller.

She could barely control her excitement as they rolled into a tiny town that she was told was her destination. "Here? Are you certain?"

"Yes, ma'am. This is Creed's Crossing. We're going to let the horses rest for an hour, if anyone would like to step out and stretch their legs." The man took her trunk off the back of the coach and left it in the road.

Zeke wasn't there to greet her. She walked up the street to the mercantile, and it was closed. A few minutes later, a young woman walked down the street.

"Hello. I'm looking for Zeke Hillerman. Do you know where I can find him?"

"Yes, his place is that last building." The woman pointed in the opposite direction.

"Thank you so much."

She almost ran down the street and to the building that had two doors. She opened the one and stepped inside. "Zeke! Zeke!"

She wandered around and realized the house wasn't quite finished, but when she went upstairs, she saw dresses, a set of combs by a hairbrush, and a dozen other items that said a woman was living there. Air went in and didn't come out. *No! No! No! Why Zeke? Why let me come this far. Why did you do this to me? You said I was your woman and that you loved me.*

She could feel the tears filling her eyes as she ran down the stairs. Stepping off the last stair, she practically ran into a young, beautiful, blonde woman whose belly told Matilda everything that she didn't want to know.

Zeke was terrible about writing letters. When she thought about it, she hadn't heard from him in probably over two months. *You found another woman. Why?* She flew out the door and into the dirt road.

Her stomach clenched. Anger, frustration, and disappointment crashed together breaking her heart and shattering her dreams. She bit back her tears and asked where the stagecoach was going.

"Northwest. We run between The Central Pacific and the Northern Pacific Railroads."

"Can I go as far as Homestead Canyon?"

"No ma'am. The closest I'll be is Hanover."

She gathered up whatever self-preservation she could muster and replied, "Excellent. Take me there."

By the time she reached Hanover, her anger had left her and she'd reconciled herself to the idea of being forced to live with her father. Except she knew in her heart that she could never go back to the soddy. She went into the livery of Hanover and asked if anyone would take her to Homestead Canyon.

A voice called. "I'll be leaving here in an hour to deliver mail if you want to come."

"Yes. That would be wonderful. Thank you."

Sam Bowmen came around the corner. "It's a two-day trip. There's a cabin along the way. I'll let you use it."

She instantly recognized the man who brought the mail to Homestead Canyon several times a week. "Thank you. That is kind of you."

That evening, Sam Bowmen put her trunk in the cabin for her. There was a pump and she filled a large basin with water. She washed up for the first time in days and it felt wonderful. And when morning came she dressed in one of her better dresses and prepared to return to the town where everyone thought she was a boy.

She pulled her freshly washed hair off her face with combs, and then managed to pull it back, making it look as though her hair had been pulled into a bun. She added her straw hat that she had used for travel and was pleased with the way she thought she looked in spite of not having a mirror.

She squared her shoulders and prepared to face the town. She also crossed her fingers that the boardinghouse would have a room for her. *I'm not going to the soddy.*

Homestead Canyon looked the same. Other than the addition of a few houses, it hadn't changed much from the first time she'd ever seen it. The driver dropped her and her trunk by the boardinghouse, and then went to the store to deliver the mail.

Mustering up her courage, she knocked on the door.

Beatrice answered with a friendly hello.

"I need a room."

"Oh dear, I don't have anything. It will be at least Friday before I will have an opening. Mr. Van Dyke has some people from the city visiting the mine." She pointed to one house.

"You might want to ask Lena if she would have a room you could use."

The name instantly brought to mind the lovely blonde woman who always wore the most beautiful dresses. "Thank you, Miz Beatrice."

"Do I know you?"

She hadn't meant to make that mistake. "Not exactly."

She turned away from the woman with rosy cheeks and out of the corner of her eye she spotted Lena. Turning back for a moment, her smile was more genuine. "Thank you, ma'am. If you don't mind, I'll leave my trunk here until I know where I'm staying, and I can send someone for it."

Matilda walked swiftly to Lena's house. "Lena." She waved. "Lena." She almost broke into a run to capture the woman's attention. "Lena!"

Lena turned and stared at Matilda.

"Lena. Please, wait a moment." She gasped trying to capture her breath. She finally made it to the house's porch and Lena looked somewhat frightened. "Lena, it's Matt."

"Matt? What's wrong? Where is he?"

Matilda giggled. "Oh, Lena, think about it. You almost guessed my secret that day you handed me your Harper's Bazaar. I'm Matt!"

Lena stared wide-eyed.

"My father kept me dressed as a boy and told everyone my name was Matt when it's actually Matilda. He was trying to protect me in a mining town filled with men when I didn't even have a mother to look after me." She heaved a sigh. "I always loved your clothes and thought you were the prettiest woman around here. I wanted to wear dresses and look like you."

"Matt?"

"Yes. I'm Matt. I promise, I'm very much a woman and always was." She couldn't hold back her giggle. "I love the dresses, but wearing shoes in the summer is killing me."

Lena crossed her arms over her chest and furrowed her brow. "If you really are Matt, what did I send you into my house last year to kill?"

"An itty bitty snake. And I refused to kill it, because they eat bugs." The memory of that day flew through her mind in a million tiny pictures. "I finally found it under a basket in your hall. Poor thing was so frightened."

"Oh, Matt it really is you. But how did you hide your…" She put her hand to her chest.

"I bound them. Oh, Lena, when I stopped doing that - they hurt! Then I swear they doubled in size." She looked down towards her toes. "I've doubled in size."

"No, you didn't. You are still the tiniest thing."

"Lena, I need help. The boardinghouse is full until Friday, is there any chance I can stay with you?"

Lena's fingertips touched her lips. "I wouldn't mind having you, but I need to discuss this with my husband before I say yes. Will you give me a few hours and come back then? It will only be until Friday?"

"That's what Miz Beatrice said."

"Let me discuss it with my family. I have a room that surely you should be able to use."

"Oh, Lena I would be so grateful. I know I could go to my father's, but I can't - I can't bring myself to stay with him in the soddy."

"Um, Matt… Mattie, your father is not alone. He's taken a woman." Lena looked around as if to be certain no one would hear her. "Were you still here when Merrill Hanson was found dead?"

"Yes. That was shortly before I left for Philadelphia."

Lena's voice was barely a notch above a whisper. "I don't like gossip, but I've heard your father has Merrill's woman living with him."

Matilda's mouth opened but no words came out. She tried again. "M-m-my father?"

Lena nodded.

"Oh, this I must see!"

Zeke returned to his house thrilled with all the things Joseph Coleman had given him. He had two beds. One was quite old but still pretty, and the other was plainer but serviceable. Both had mattresses. But his real excitement was over what had once been a desk. Joseph said when his oldest son married a young woman named Lydia, she had several things she had brought with her including two fancy cabinets with glass fronts. Lydia didn't particularly like the cabinets so the actual cabinet portion was used for something else and the upper, glassed cases were sent to the attic. Those two, glassed pieces would make the ends of a large desk since the desk's legs had been used for something else. There were three chairs that would work for his office and a table and two sturdy wooden unmatched chairs that could be used in the kitchen.

There were also several wooden barrels filled with odd building parts such as a set of exterior hinges, a latch, several vent covers, an old transom, and a few doorknobs. Everything was usable and would cut his expenses. With a desk, he could erect his sign, and with luck, he'd gain a few clients.

Piece by piece he carried the smaller items into the house and left the bed pieces propped against the wall. He'd take them upstairs after he was done setting up his desk. Ruth was nowhere to be found and he figured she was sleeping. The bigger she became the more she wanted to sleep. He would have worried about her, but he noticed that his two cows that were heavy with calves seemed to be less active. *As long as Ruth doesn't have her baby while she's here alone with me.*

Zeke moved the chairs in his office into position and then arranged the glass-fronted pieces. It was one thing to carry the heavy desktop and another thing to try and lift it high enough to sit on top of the two pieces of furniture. He finally stood the top on its end and lowered it onto the one cabinet before sliding it into place over the other cabinet. All the pieces were cut from maple but they didn't exactly match in style. He walked around the desk three times and studied it. *It looks...*

hmm, maybe… decent. That's the word - decent. They look decent together. No one will fault me for being frugal.

He put the nicest of the three chairs behind the desk. In the barrels, he knew he had four wooden wheels he could use on the chair. *I'll do that tomorrow.*

Rummaging around, he found the ledger and the pen and ink set that Mr. Haas had given him. He put the pen set on his desk and placed the ledger in the small desk drawer. With wheels on his chair, the room would be perfect.

Ruth still hadn't appeared so he began to take the beds upstairs. That's when he discovered that Ruth wasn't there. He put the pretty bed in his bedroom, knowing that Mattie would be thrilled. It was tall with a carved canopy that would hold mosquito netting.

He stood for a moment and envisioned Mattie's naked body in his bed. The netting would add an ethereal ambiance to the scene. He groaned. Mattie caused him to lose sleep as it was, and he knew he needed to write and tell her to come. He was almost ready for her.

He wondered if they could marry in the little church in town. It wouldn't be fancy. Maybe Ruth would make them a cake.

His thoughts returned to Mattie's milky-white skin that was dusted in gold. *So beautiful!* He imagined running his hands over her skin and kissing every inch of her body. He walked out of the house and far across the pasture to a place where no one would see him. His feelings for her burned deep inside of him. He closed his eyes, as he imagined touching his lips to hers and then drifting lower over her petite body. *I love you, Mattie.*

He dropped to his knees as his body reacted to his thoughts. *Oh, Mattie! Oh!* His body burned until the sensation caused him to explode. He turned and rolled onto his back in the grass and watched the nearly cloudless sky until he found some composure.

When he walked into the house, he called Ruth. Still no answer. He took the other bed to her room and put the pieces together. *She'll be happy that she's no longer sleeping on a pallet.*

Hunger caused him to cook something. He found a tin of oats and added them to some boiling water. There was a jar of sorghum syrup and he figured he'd pour some of that on his oats. Then he wondered if he'd used too much water.

Ruth came through the kitchen door with a big smile. "I had the most wonderful visit with Virginia Barrett. She says Cheyenne will be the perfect place for a mill. She has family all through the South."

Zeke lifted the lid on the cooking oats and stirred them again. He really didn't care to listen to Ruth's prater. She droned on about fabric and things that didn't interest him. Then suddenly she stopped.

"Where did you find this awful table?" She wrinkled her nose.

"It's not terrible and until I can earn more money, it is a place to sit in the kitchen."

"It's ugly. Looks like trail furniture."

"No. Apparently it is merely well used."

"Why don't you simply order a few things?"

He swallowed the bile that rose in his throat. "You seem to think that I can walk into the corral and pick up money by the fistful. I've spent what I had building this place."

She waved her hand in front of her face. "Go to bank and borrow some money."

"I'm not going to spend what I don't have. Our parents taught us that. Did you fail to learn that lesson?"

Ruth huffed. "Some woman came here today. She walked into the house as though she owned it. Strange thing is, she never said a word and just took off. Left on the stagecoach."

Something in Zeke's chest tightened. "What did she look like?"

Ruth looked up and acted as though everything she wanted to know was written on the ceiling of the kitchen. "Beige and brown traveling dress, straw hat, copper colored hair pulled off her face into what looked like a loose bun, she was quite petite, plain, and covered with freckles."

"Mattie!"

"If it was Mattie, why didn't she stay?"

"I have no idea. Which way did the coach leave?"

Ruth turned as if to face the front door and the pointed northward. "That way."

Zeke took the stairs two at a time. He rolled a few clothes into a blanket and ran down the stairs. "I'm going after her."

"Not until you eat that mess you've made in the kitchen."

Zeke had lost his appetite, but he knew he had a long ride ahead and needed food in his stomach. He gobbled every speck of the oats. It was gummy from too much water but that didn't matter to him. A spoonful of sorghum syrup sweetened it. He grabbed a few jars of food from the kitchen pantry and told Ruth to stay put until he returned. "I'm taking Shep with me."

He saddled both horses and called to Shep. *The only place for her to go is Homestead Canyon. She has to be there!*

Dawn was breaking when he stopped for a nap. When he awakened, he rode until he couldn't stay awake any longer. He did that until he reached Hanover. On the far side of town, he stopped long enough to take a nap and to wash up in the river. *At least the days haven't been scalding hot.*

Since he wasn't driving a cart or herding animals, he figured he could make the trip in a few hours, if the horses were up to it.

He stopped by a creek long enough to let the horses drink, have a little grass, and rest. Shep stretched out and panted. He knew he had pushed the animals to the max and guilt crawled over him. It wasn't their fault Mattie had run off and that he wanted her back. The day was warm and the sky was a cloudless blue dome over his head. He pulled out his pocket watch and checked the time. At ten forty-seven in the morning, the sun still hadn't reached the apex and he knew he had quite a ways to go.

Certain that he wasn't more than a few more hours from Homestead Canyon, he wanted to push onward and not stagnate next to a creek, but when he called to Shep, the dog didn't budge.

"Don't tell me you are too tired to push onward." He sat next to the dog and checked his paws and legs.

The dog made a soft growl and moved under a fir tree.

"What is wrong with you, Shep? Why are you acting so peculiar?"

Zeke heard the whoosh and saw the arrow land inches from where he was sitting. The hair on his nape prickled and every sinew in his body tightened. He had a pistol on his hip and the rifle was on the horse. But alone against a band of Indians with almost no cover, the odds were against him. Then he remembered Mattie's friend Gray Fox. If that was the band of Indians, he didn't have a prayer of a chance of surviving. They were skilled hunters, and if Mattie was angry with him… They would side with her. He waited. Another arrow came whooshing by his shoulder and another and then another. Each one could have easily hit him but whoever was doing it intended to scare him. *They're doing a good job.*

He sat motionless. Then a spear landed less than an inch from his hand. He'd had enough and realized he couldn't continue to sit like a target. He slowly wrapped his fingers around the spear and stood. "What do you want?"

Another arrow flew past his left ear, but this time he could hear the snap of the string. "Gray Fox, if that is you, I'm going to turn you over my knee and show you what white people do when their children misbehave."

"Try it, Zeke."

Slowly Zeke turned in the direction of the voice, and faced a man who wore nothing but a loincloth and several feathers in his hair. The young man had grown tall and broad of chest.

High cheekbones went to points below the eyes and under that he had dimples. If it had not been for the distinctive cheekbones and dimples, Zeke would have never recognized the man. "You've grown up since I saw you last."

"Where's Matt."

"I was going to ask you that question. I'm hoping she's in Homestead Canyon."

"Why there? You sent her away, yet you look for her here?"

Zeke tried to explain what he knew, and Gray Fox shook his head.

"Come with me. Help me find her."

"You want me to ride through the town with you?"

"Yes. If we are together, people will accept you. Many of your tribe are scouts. You need to give the white man a chance."

"We gave them a chance. They make treaties with us and then they break them."

"That's the government, that is not individuals. I'm sure some people will run in fear and others will not like you, but they will learn to trust you."

Gray Fox pushed his lips outward. "They think I will scalp them and kill their children."

"Show them that you won't."

Zeke was certain that he'd not totally convinced Gray Fox that he would be safe, but together they rode into Homestead Canyon. Shep followed but he seemed leery of the man with all the feathers as though Gray Fox was a giant bird. They tethered their horses and began to walk together through the tiny town, hoping to spot Mattie.

"Thank you, Miz Beatrice."

Zeke heard her voice and turned around. Then it dawned on him that he was looking for Matt and not Matilda. He spotted a woman in a fancy yellow dress with a straw hat. Red curls hid her nape.

"Mattie!"

The young woman turned and stared in their direction. Her face lit up and she hurried to them. "Gray Fox!" She threw her arms around the Indian. "I've missed you so much!"

A pang of jealousy ran through Zeke. "Mattie. Why did you run away?"

She turned to Zeke. "How dare you even ask me that! You bring me out here only to find out you have a wife."

"You think Ruth is my wife? She's my oldest sister. Her husband went to find a town where he can build a mill for our wool."

"Oh, tell me anything since you have me here. I'm not stupid. I know what I saw, and I'm not about to believe something because the person telling me the tall tale is a man."

"Mattie, you're beautiful."

"Don't think you can sweet talk me into leaving." She took Gray Fox's hand. "You've grown so tall."

"And you are so little."

She playfully smacked his arm and then realized they had a crowd of people around them. Squaring her shoulders, she turned to the crowd. "This is Gray Fox. He was my childhood playmate. No one told me he was an Indian or that I should be afraid, so I wasn't. Sometimes I would sneak off and visit his family. They are like any family here. Don't be afraid of my friend."

She turned to Gray Fox. "Are you married?"

He shook his head. "My mother wants to me to take Silver Sky, but I do not want her. She is too…I forget the word. Always telling everyone around her what to do."

Mattie giggled. "Demanding?"

"Yes. I'm tired of being told things. I'm tired of the constant trouble with the Army. I want to pick one spot and not be moved."

"I could use help with the ranch." Zeke offered.

"What do you do on the ranch?"

"It is my ranch. I'm starting so it will be mostly sheep, cows for milk, and chickens for eggs."

"No hunting?"

"Maybe for fun, but I will raise our food."

"I would like that."

Zeke turned to Mattie. "I love you. I told you a long time ago that you were my woman. Ruth is my sister and you must believe me. I will send a telegram to my mother if you want. Will you believe her?"

She put a hand to her forehead. "I am here, and there are things I must do while I am here."

"Let's start with the telegram." He turned to the store and then to Mattie. "If I can prove that Ruth is my sister will you please marry me and return to Creed's Crossing with me?"

She chewed on her bottom lip for a moment. "Will you let me stay here for a few days? I need to talk to my father and visit with a few people. Furthermore, I feel like Gray Fox. I don't want anyone demanding things of me or trying to order me around."

Zeke nodded. But a little voice inside of him said she wasn't going to go to Creed's Crossing.

NINE

Zeke looked around. "If you are going to be here, then I'll go to the Haas stockyard. I'll be back in exactly one week. You should have your answer to the telegram by then."

"That's fair enough. I'll be staying with a friend tonight and tomorrow night and then I will be at the boardinghouse."

Zeke reached in his pocket and withdrew the pouch where he kept his money. "Here. You will need money to stay here."

"I don't need your money."

"Take it anyway."

She took the money and walked away from them.

Gray Fox snickered. "She always have a hard mind and been filled with fire."

"I think you are right. And what about you? Do you want to come with me?"

"I will go back and tell my family. They will be upset, but they will celebrate my new life."

"Do you understand one week?"

"Yes. I know the white man's calendar."

"Then I will meet you here." Zeke mounted his horse. "Next time, do not shoot arrows at me."

"I scare you?"

Zeke turned and grinned. "What do you think?"

"You were worse than your dog."

Zeke laughed and turned towards the Haas stockyard. "See you in a week."

He didn't need both horses, so he left one at the livery behind Mr. Van Dyke's house. Traveling with only his horse and Shep, he made good time and arrived at the Haas property during the night. Rather than disturbing anyone, he slept under the stars and as dawn broke he went to the house and knocked on the kitchen door. "Any chance a hungry cowboy and his dog could have a little breakfast?"

Cook opened the door and squealed with delight. She threw her arms around him and dragged him into the house. "You stink worse than a pig's sty. Let me heat some water for a bath."

A few minutes later, he was soaking in the hot tub. Any other time, he would have complained that the water was too hot for a summer day, but every part of his body ached and he was grateful for the luxury.

Scrubbed clean and shaved, he went into the kitchen and was sent to the dining room. Little Suzanne flew to him and

Phyllis joined the fun for a big hug.

"You haven't given up your dream of a ranch, have you?" Mr. Haas asked.

"Not at all." During breakfast, he told of all that he had accomplished and didn't quite tell everything when it came to Mattie. "She wanted to see her dad and some old friends. With luck we'll marry and head to my place."

"Oh, a wedding." Mrs. Haas looked at her husband. "Why don't you send for the minister in Gilmore and we could have the wedding here. Wouldn't that be lovely?"

Mr. Haas grinned at his wife and then at Zeke. "Do you think your future wife would object?"

Zeke rolled his palms up. "There's a tiny church in Creed's Crossing, but I guess it would be better if we were married before we left. I'm to meet her in one week."

"Oh my, that doesn't give us much time. I must send invitations to our friends in Hanover and surrounding ranches."

"While my wife makes all the plans, let us go to my office, and we shall discuss your progress on the ranch."

Don't turn you back on me, Mattie. I love you. But that little negative voice inside of him wouldn't be quiet.

Matilda spent the next two days with Lena. They joked and laughed and had a wonderful time. Lena was thrilled to know that Matilda had learned to use the sewing machine. Matilda showed Lena how to bead and how to mix beading with embroidery.

Lena always wore the latest styles of clothing and she knew all the proper society customs. So many things were different from what Zeke's mom did. Apparently things on the outskirts of Philadelphia were more low-keyed, yet many were the same.

Matilda didn't want to let on that she'd had a problem with Zeke, and she crossed her fingers that Ruth really was Zeke's sister. But the feeling of being betrayed wouldn't go away.

Lena was an immaculate housekeeper and an excellent cook. She talked about the seafood dishes that were common in her hometown, and although they sounded delicious, Matilda knew she'd probably never taste shrimp or scallops. But when Lena made something called Tea Cakes, Matilda wanted the recipe. Matilda carefully wrote down several recipes that Lena gave her, including the delicate biscuits that were so delicious with tea.

"Have you been to see Rosalind since you've returned?"

"I've seen a few people, but no one, other than you, knows that I was once Matt."

"We must make the rounds. I can't wait to see the looks on a few faces. You certainly surprised me."

They went to see Rosalind at the house, but Lola greeted them. Matilda told Lola who she was. Lola's eyes lit up as she grabbed at Matilda and hugged her.

Lena and Matilda went to the company store and there in the back of the store, hidden by a display shelf, was Rosalind sitting at the desk.

"Excuse me." For some reason, her courage suddenly left.

Rosalind was an important person in this town. "Miz Rosalind, I'm not certain that you will recognize me. I used to run errands for the store, and sometimes use your dictionary. You always wondered why I was interested in things that most normal boys weren't… that's because I wasn't a boy. My father hid me in an attempt to protect me in a town filled with men."

"Matt?"

"It's actually Matilda. Zeke Hillerman discovered my secret and sent me to live with his parents in the Philadelphia area."

"Zeke?" She cocked her head to the side and narrowed her eyes as if she were trying to remember the name.

"He was the blond man who used to deliver animals from the Haas stockyard."

"Ah, yes. I remember him. He left a few months ago and now another man does it."

"He left to start his own ranch. He bought the land and built a house for us." As soon as the words came out of her mouth, she realized what she had said, and the pride that she felt when she said those words. Then she felt that stab of betrayal.

"Oh, Matt, um Matilda, I'm so happy for you. I wish a thousand blessings on you and Zeke."

"Thank you." Matilda smiled. "We will probably need every one of those. I thought when I came back that it would be easy for us. But it's like starting from the beginning, as if we never knew each other."

"Certainly you've kept in touch during your absence."

"For ten months, I wrote him at least three times a week. He wrote to me only a few times."

"Men!" Rosalind held her hands up. "But at least you know who he is. That is more than I knew about Mr. Van Dyke." She smiled sweetly. "Mr. Van Dyke's a wonderful man, and I couldn't ask for a better or a more handsome husband."

Matilda shook her head. "I heard you were a mail-order bride, but I couldn't believe that you would marry a man you didn't know."

"The agency I was with was very careful about placement. I knew quite a bit about him, but I didn't know him."

"Zeke and I have a few details to work out before I consent to marriage."

"Well, I think Zeke is going to marry a very special person. I have no idea how you managed to pretend that you were a boy for so long or how you hid your feminine beauty."

"Thank you. Sometimes it was easy and sometimes it was hard. Once you came with your pretty dresses, and then Lena came, I wanted to scream that I was a girl, and I wanted to dress as one. Well, I wanted to dress like you and have tea parties and invite my friends."

"Ma-Matilda, that's a wonderful idea. I'll have a tea party for you with cake, and I'll invite all the women in Homestead Canyon."

"Even Yanyu? I think she suspected I was a girl."

"Yes, all the women. If you were staying longer, I would order a big batch of lemons from San Francisco for lemonade. We'll have to make do with tea. It will be so much fun!" Rosalind grinned. "I will admit I miss Matt. I could have handed him all the invitations and he would have delivered each one in probably less than an hour. He was so reliable."

Matilda's laugh bubbled. "Those days are over! You are not getting me back into a pair of pants or getting me to bind my… you know." She touched her hand to her chest.

Rosalind's jaw dropped. "That's what you did?"

Matilda nodded. "And those special times. I think Yanyu saw me washing for she would wander up the creek to do the same thing."

"Oh, Matilda, how awful." Lena pushed some tears from her cheeks. "I wish you had confided in me. I feel so terrible for not paying more attention. I thought maybe you were a boy with certain inclinations…"

Matilda sucked in a breath. "Oh, no. Um, no. That I had the desire to do something…"

"I'm so sorry. That was a terrible thing to think."

Matilda shook her head. "I don't think you were alone. My father had warned me about such men. In the last few months I was here, there were several men leering at me. I wasn't certain if they figured out I was a female or they thought I was a willing male. I had to leave. I had to go away. I was scared."

"Have you seen your father since you've been back?" Rosalind asked.

Matilda looked at Rosalind and then at Lena. "I need to do that. I need to face him and tell him the truth. I left so quickly with my brother. I never even wrote to him. Every time I started to write, I tore up my letter. I need to see him." She bit at her lower lip. "I hear he's living with a woman."

Rosalind nodded. "Merrill Hanson's widow, Abigail. She seems much happier with your father."

"My father is a good man. It took my leaving here for me to realize it. He's a little rough around the edges, but he's a decent, God-fearing man who did his best to raise me without a mother. Does it make sense if I say he was a lousy father and ten times worse as a mother, but he did *his* best and tried hard?"

Rosalind hugged Matilda. "Yes, it makes perfect sense. Go see him and tell him that you still love him. Lena and I have a party to plan!"

Zeke thought he'd be working in the stockyard, but instead, Mr. Haas mentored Zeke the entire time. He sent him to meet Marc Pole who ran a successful sheep ranch.

Marc was interested in the wool mill and gave Zeke quite a few names of others who were raising sheep instead of cattle. "The cattle boon is over. We can barely sell for three dollars per hundredweight. I still keep a few head with the hopes that the market will turn around, but I think it's over. The winter of '86 and the drought that followed did us in. I lost over twenty-five percent of my herd. They ate the bark off the trees and killed the trees on my property. I can't afford another such loss."

Zeke knew he'd made the right decision. Plus, there was no doubt in his mind that sheep were more intelligent and easier to handle than cattle. They also didn't require the same care. He'd either have to learn to sheer them or hire someone to do it. And from what Marc said, hiring someone was cheaper and easier. Marc wrote down the name of a man who came up from Colorado to shear the sheep.

Marc offered to sell Zeke some sheep, but Zeke turned him down. "But I'd be very interested in one of those female pups. Shep is getting older and I think he'd appreciate a little help."

Marc laughed. "If he only wanted help, you'd have asked for a male."

Zeke chuckled. "I wasn't thinking along those lines, but I'm certain Shep will appreciate a pretty gal when they aren't working."

At four months of age, Tricks was full of energy and had already had some training. But when she tried to herd Shep, he put her in her place.

Zeke laughed. "You two will have to work it out."

Tricks was a beauty with blue eyes and a coat that was more white and silver, than Shep's mostly black coat. She had one ear that flopped down, which gave her an endearing quality when she'd look at a human. She'd also cost him more than he had wanted to spend. But Marc said her mom and dad had both come from Scotland and had a long history of herding sheep. Apparently Marc's wife's family was still in Scotland.

Zeke could feel his confidence growing, except when it came to Mattie. *If she has any clue that the Haases are planning our wedding... Please, Mattie, I love you. I built the library that you wanted. I'd do anything for you. Anything!*

Matilda smiled at Roscoe Jones who ran the company store. "Do you have any ham steaks?"

He found four. They weren't very big but they would be enough. She knew her father loved them. Then she checked the shelves, found several canned vegetables, and asked for a bag of potatoes and some butter. She hoped Abigail Hanson knew how to cook everything.

As she paid for the items she said, "I'll be back for them in ten minutes."

She scooted to the boardinghouse and asked if by any chance Beatrice had any cookies or something that resembled dessert.

"I just finished frying a batch of fresh doughnuts. How many do you want?"

"A half dozen would be good." Matilda paid for them. Then returned to the store for the other things she had purchased. She carried the heavy load to the soddy and then discovered she couldn't knock with so much in her arms. "Abigail!"

The woman answered the door looking more than a little frightened.

"I'm Matilda Berwyn. I've come to see my father."

"He's still at the mine."

The groceries were heavy and Matilda was certain she'd drop everything if she didn't put them down. She pushed past Abigail and set everything on the table. The little soddy looked better. Abigail had hung curtains at the one window and the table looked different. There were also chairs.

"Supper. I hate to impose, but I bought my father's favorite foods. Would you like help fixing everything?"

Wordlessly Abigail began to sort though the items.

"Abigail, I don't bite. I heard you were here and from the looks of things - the place is nicer."

The mine's whistle blew and it startled Matilda. "I haven't heard that sound in almost a year, but I come back and I jump every time I hear it."

"Who are you?"

"It's a long story, but you knew me as Matt." She explained the situation and Abigail nodded.

"You plannin' on eatin' here?"

"I bought enough so that I could."

"You wantin' all this fixed?"

Matilda shook her head. "It's probably too much."

Matilda sat at the table and watched Abigail. She was skinny with an odd tummy bulge. Her front teeth were broken but they had been that way for some time. *Did Merrill do that to you?* She was a dark blonde with hazel eyes – more brown than hazel, but even in the low light of the soddy, Matilda could see the blue-green flecks in them.

Matilda summoned her courage. "Are you with child?"

The woman stopped and turned. "I not tell anyone."

Matilda couldn't hold back her laughter. "I'm going to have a baby brother or sister. All those years I wanted one, and just my luck, when I won't be around, I'll have one." She stood and looked in the pantry box. "May I make some coffee?"

"Yes'um."

"Where are you from?"

"Georgia. My daddy gots killed durin' the war. Mamma moved me to Texas and my husband moved me here. But him died."

"I know. Is my father good to you? Does he take good care of you and treat you right?" Matilda poured water from the jug into a pan. "Is this from the creek or the pump?"

"It's from the pump. Your daddy is a mighty fine man. He treats me likes I's the belle of the ball."

"I think my father missed my mother, but for whatever reason, he never looked for another woman when I was around. You want me to peel some potatoes?"

With the potatoes boiling, the two women sat at the table together and chatted. Abigail was barely twelve when her mother handed her over to Merrill Hanson. For over twenty years, she'd been mistreated. At least Matilda's father was kind to Abigail, and she obviously loved him. Any guilt that Matilda had carried for killing Merrill Hanson was gone. She had apparently done Abigail a huge favor.

Abigail fixed a big tub of warm water.

Matilda's father walked through the door. He stopped and stared at Matilda. "You're back?"

"Only for a few days. I'll assume that's your bath water so I'll step outside. When dinner is ready, call me."

She walked around behind the soddy and discovered a small garden that Abigail was tending. Life had changed for all of them, and Matilda knew she wanted to be with Zeke, but there was this niggling little doubt that she couldn't ignore. She tried to remember the names on the quilt she had made. There were two more sisters who had married and moved away. *But why would his sister be living with him?*

Abigail called Matilda for dinner. Her father was scrubbed clean and shaven. This time he hugged her, and she could tell he was fighting tears.

They ate their supper, and afterwards Matilda stepped outside with her father. She told him about her life in Germantown, and that she had returned because she wanted him to know that she really did love him. But she also resented being treated like a boy, yet she understood. She decided to leave out the part about killing Merrill Hanson.

He seemed pleased that she'd taken her exams. "You always were smart like your mom. Never saw a woman who read as much as she did, but I think you read more."

"Thanks. I brought you something… While you were working, I used to play in the creek. I found some gold. Not much and eventually I quit finding it. I promise, I looked hard for more. I dug through that creek bed. I went upstream and downstream looking for more and there was nothing. Just a few nuggets, but I cashed them in and got some money." She reached into her pocket and pulled out a little bag. She undid the drawstring and reached inside. "There's enough here for you to buy a house and more. I think it's time for you and Abigail to start over. I guess it doesn't matter if you stay here. Mr. Van Dyke is a good man and he treats you well."

"I have more experience in a mine than anyone up there. He knows it, and he relies on me more than the others. I even got a raise."

"That's wonderful." She put the money into his hand. "Mr. Van Dyke knows I found gold and where I found it. He doesn't know how much I found. But he'll believe you if you tell him I gave you money. Take care of Abigail. She loves you." Matilda swiped at her tears. "I'm staying at the boardinghouse for the next few days. After that, I'm not certain if I'm going to Creed's Crossing, Wyoming, or if I'll go back to Philadelphia."

He thumbed the money. "This is a lot of money. How much did you find?"

She smiled at her father. "Enough for me to be comfortable and to give you some. Give me a minute alone with Abigail, and then I'll leave."

She walked back inside and Abigail had already cleaned up the supper dishes. "I want you to have this. Buy yourself a pretty dress or two, and maybe a few things for the baby." She gave the woman several dollars and a hug. "Take good care of my father. He needs it."

Fighting tears, Matilda headed for the boardinghouse.

That night she stared at the ceiling and wondered what she was going to do. How many places needed a librarian?

In the morning, it seemed as though the entire town was buzzing over the party at the Van Dyke's. Beatrice was in the kitchen making cakes. Mr. Jones was even washing the windows at the company store. It appeared as though half the women in town were down by the stream washing clothes. *Anything for a party.*

She thought back to the going-away party that Mrs.

Hillerman had and who all had come. Something inside of her saw the humor in the situation and began to giggle. Nothing about her had really changed. Not one freckled moved or went away. She was still who she always was. The only difference was this time she wore a dress and acted like a female. Except she was being treated as though she were royalty.

Then she remembered the party Miz Rosalind had to welcome Beatrice. This party would be different from what Mrs. Hillerman had hosted.

She sat on the edge of the porch of the boardinghouse and looked out over the town. *I'm no one special. We are all so bored with our lives that any excuse to dress up and socialize is an escape. And I'm not going to sit here and be bored!*

She ran upstairs to the room she had rented and changed into a plain dress. It was an ivory-colored cotton, and it didn't have a bustle, but it did have a beautiful border of colorful flowers on the hem and on the sleeves. She dropped a wide-brimmed straw hat on her head that was trimmed with ribbon and checked her image in the mirror. Satisfied, she went down the stairs, out the front door, and then down the town's little street before cutting across the field to the stream. She pulled off her shoes and discovered that her feet had become tender.

Every scratchy blade of grass, pebble, etc. was felt as she stepped, but she didn't care. She followed the stream until the town had vanished and continued onward to her golden spot. Lifting her hem, she flicked through the stones of the creek's bed looking for anything that might be gold. Finding nothing she sloshed her way onward until the creek ran faster and the stones protruded out of the water.

Several times she stopped and looked for gold. She continued upstream until she reached an area that was filled with large rocks, the sort that she could sit on and not worry about getting wet by the rushing water. Once settled, she looked around her. *How could anyone be bored when surrounded by nature?*

She watched a bee darting between some black-eyed Susan flowers. The fast flowing water obscured the sounds of the birds and every other noise around her. In the open field, there was a doe and her baby. She watched as they made their way to the stream and then stopped for a drink not more than twenty feet from her.

Suddenly they took off, and as she was about to turn to see what had frightened them, a spear landed near her, fell over and began to flow downstream. A young male chased after his spear. It bounced between the rocks and then floated briskly. As soon as the boy retrieved it, he ran to her. She held her arms open to him as he climbed to where she was sitting.

"Little Wind Runner, are you learning to hunt?"

The child smiled at her and then tugged on her skirt.

"Yes, I'm wearing dresses these days. Where is your brother?"

He never answered, he only wiggled closer to her.

"You have not learned our language." She put her arm around him and hugged him.

He smiled brightly.

In a few more moments, she spotted the other men. They

rode to her, and she waved her hello.

Gray Fox's father reprimanded his youngest son for throwing a spear at Matilda.

She helped the young boy step down from his perch beside her and she followed. Once on dry land, she hugged the father and greeted the other members of the hunting party.

"Don't be hard on him. He's only doing what his brother does to me."

"Yes, but his brother knows how to throw. Little Wind Runner might hit you."

"And where is Gray Fox?"

The father pressed his lips together. "The Army caught him."

"Oh, no! Is he arrested?"

The man furrowed his brow. "We have seen him several times and he is not in shackles. We think they want him as a scout."

"He wanted to come with me."

"We know. We did not want him leaving the tribe, but going with you would have been preferable to being taken by the Army."

She looked up at Gray Fox's father and smiled. "If he is at the fort, then I will write to him there. He is valuable to them because he knows our language."

"You leave Homestead Canyon?"

"Yes. We are going to Creed's Crossing, Wyoming. We will be on Lakota hunting grounds."

"You must be careful. We know you, but our brothers do not."

She nodded. "You tell your brothers that we are good people."

"Yes, but like other white men, you take our land and put up fences."

"You tell them that we will share and we will hunt with them. We will cause them no harm."

Gray Fox's father shook his head. "It is not that simple, my child."

She hugged Gray Fox's father and said goodbye to the other men, as a few tears silently rolled down her cheeks. She knew she'd never see these people again. *Stay safe, Gray Fox, don't let them hurt you.*

The following morning she saw Sam Bowmen pull into Homestead Canyon with his mail cart. She waved a friendly hello and he waved back.

She wandered into the company store, thinking that a sassafras candy stick would taste good.

"Good to see you, Matilda. You saved me from having to find you." Roscoe Jones instantly handed her a telegram.

She looked at it and smiled.

Ruth & Naomi sisters STOP

That was all she needed to know. Now she only wondered why Ruth was in Creed's Crossing and staying at Zeke's house.

When the following morning came, she decided on a peachy-pink dress. She loved the color on her. The skirt was ruched, as were the sleeves, and a pretty pink bow draped the bustle. At first, she balked at lace with an ivory tint. Certain it made some things look dirty and old, but slowly she realized the color was better on her than pure white. She grabbed her cotton, ecru-colored crocheted shawl and was pleased with the effect.

Every so often the Reverend Ritter would come to Homestead Canyon and this was that Sunday. She ate a light breakfast and then went over to the church. Abigail was already there, but not Matilda's father. Matilda walked to where Abigail was sitting, smiled, and took the spot next to her. "Hello."

Abigail smiled.

Matilda knew that by sitting next to Abigail it showed the town acceptance of her father's situation. She leaned over and whispered, "Make Pa marry you."

Abigail grinned. "He was going to do it this Sunday, but he had to work. I'm hoping Reverend Ritter will do it tonight when your father gets off from work."

Matilda listened to the reverend and tried not to wiggle from boredom in her seat. It seemed he did virtually the same sermon each time he came. When the sermon was over, she was more than pleased. Often the man was repetitive, and this was one of those Sunday sermons. Besides she had other things on her mind.

After church, Matilda went to Rosalind's house for her party.

"Come in, Matilda, I adore your dress."

"Thank you. I fell in love with it and bought it at Wanamaker's in Philadelphia. They had all sorts of beautiful clothes, and I knew I'd never be able to sew such a dress."

Rosalind clapped her hands together once. "You've been to Wanamaker's? You must tell me all about it!"

"Did I hear someone say Wanamaker's?" Lena came into parlor from the dining room. "I want to hear all about it, too!"

Matilda told them about the beautiful building, and all the wonderful things under its roof. "They are building an even bigger one!"

Rosalind shook her head. "I can't imagine such a big store even though I've seen the advertisements for them." She motioned for Lena and Matilda to follow her. "You must come and see the food we've prepared."

Matilda walked into the dining room and she was surprised. There were little slices of beef tucked into small rolls and there were slices of ham on a platter, and several vegetables in bowls. But on a table, all by itself, was a beautiful cake with a drizzled sugar icing on it. She could smell the ginger, clove, and mace in it. She knew Rosalind considered this afternoon tea as a very special occasion for such a risen cake was a rare treat.

Lena sighed. "I must go home for a few minutes. I'm afraid Robert will wake up from his nap, and John won't know what to do."

Matilda smiled. *Someday I want a baby.* "Go. I want to play with him when he's ready for a visit." She turned to Rosalind. "Is little Peter Junior napping?"

"Yes."

"Oh, this will be a fun afternoon with all the babies."

Rosalind laughed. "Wait until you have your own."

"To me, this is having all the fun without all the hard work."

The afternoon party went beautifully. So many of the women swore they had no idea that Matt was a really a female and a few said they suspected.

Yanyu smiled and said she knew Matt was a girl. "I keep secret."

Matilda smiled. "Yes. You did. Thank you."

Matilda wanted to sample everything. She had worn her corset and didn't have room for much of anything, but she was determined to save room for a piece of that cake.

Abigail stood nearby and since everyone was around, Matilda thought she'd announce her father's intention. She winked at Abigail and took her hand. "Apparently, my father had plans for this afternoon, but he had to work. That postponed his plans until this evening. Abigail and my father are getting married."

Everyone started clapping and Abigail turned three shades of red.

"I'm thrilled for Abigail and especially for my father who has been a widower for way too long. Maybe if Abigail had been part of our lives sooner I wouldn't have had to pretend to be a boy."

There was more clapping and some cheering.

"Oh a wedding! I love weddings. I need to hurry back and see what special treat I can make for the wedding couple." Beatrice announced. "Everyone come to the boardinghouse after dinner to wish the newlyweds well."

Ruby called, "I'm going to decorate the meetinghouse so it really does look like a wedding. Anyone want to help me gather some flowers? And I'll need a few vases."

Miz Della Garfield answered, "I have several vases you may use."

"I gather flowers," Yanyu offered.

Beatrice left in haste, and that triggered several other women to also say goodbye. Many said they would stop at the church tonight for the wedding of Abigail and Matilda's father. Matilda was pleased that the afternoon went well, and that Abigail was being accepted instead of being ostracized as a fallen woman.

Matilda offered to help clean up, but Rosalind shooed her away.

Lena asked, "Does Abigail have anything special to wear for her wedding?"

"I don't think so, why?"

"I have a dress… I don't know why I still have it. It doesn't fit. I had considered having it remade into something else, but it's… I can't even see it being used as a baby dress. I was wondering if Abigail would like to wear it for her wedding. It's old-fashioned with a high waist."

"I can take it to her and ask."

"Give me one moment and we can walk to my place."

It didn't take Lena more than a few minutes to find the gown and give it to Matilda.

"Oh it's lovely."

"Do you think she can wear it or would even want to wear it? The design is Spanish with its tiers of lace."

"I know she had nothing special to wear." Matilda held the very pale yellow dress in front of her. "Well, she's taller and thinner than you, so I think it will fit. I'll take it to her now. Oh, Lena, this is so kind of you. I have a feeling she's going to be thrilled."

"Every woman wants to be—deserves to be—beautiful on her wedding day."

Matilda took the dress to Abigail and she was, as predicted, elated.

Then Matilda hurried back to the boardinghouse. Beatrice was baking a pound cake and was setting up for coffee and tea.

Beatrice moved the cups as though trying for the perfect arrangement. "I don't think we'll have as many people tonight."

"I agree. And I'm still full from my party. I'm going to go pick some more flowers."

"Yes. That would be perfect for the table."

Okay, I was thinking about Abigail. I wish I could have a wedding with friends.

TEN

Matilda cut across the meadow and strolled to the river. There, along the stream, black-eyed Susans and daisies bloomed. She picked every pretty one she could find and then picked little blue button flowers. Wandering downstream, she spotted another stand of flowers and had to cross the bridge to pick them. Then she almost didn't manage to pick what she wanted, as the ground was a little wet where they grew. But they were such a bright yellow and would look so pretty with the dress.

She picked all of them and brought everything back to the boardinghouse.

Beatrice found a vase and then a tiny vase. "Think we can use this for the flowers that she carries?"

"I was thinking the same thing and wondering what you

were planning to do with such a small vase. I have some green ribbon that might cover the vase, but it's very narrow."

"I think I have some ribbon we can use." Beatrice arranged the majority of the flowers in the large vase for the table. Then she vanished upstairs for a moment before taking the remaining flowers and making a bouquet that Abigail could carry. "I do hope your father treats her well. Merrill Henson was a horrible man. I still think someone killed him, and I've wondered if she finally found enough backbone to do it."

"I don't think she'd hurt a thing. She's way too timid. But I do know that my pa is happy. I can see it in his face. He probably thought he shouldn't have a wife while we were there – that it would hurt our image of our mother. I wish he had remarried. I could have used a mother."

Beatrice finished wrapping the flowers and the petite vase in the green ribbon. "There. It's perfect. Well, not really, but as perfect as I can make it. No one will know there's a small vase under the ribbon."

"I think it looks lovely. Abigail is going to be so pleased."

"Did you happen to tell her that she was to come here after the wedding?"

"Yes, I told her that there's a reception planned, but I think she's waiting for my father to say yes."

"Oh, no. Do you think he'd refuse?"

"Not a chance!" Matilda waved her hand through the air. "Pa isn't going to tell me no, and he's going to do anything he can to make Abigail happy."

"Abigail isn't the only wife who's been abused."

"Oh, I know. I know what I saw when making deliveries and I know probably more than I should." She shook her head. "Women feel trapped. They have no place to go, no place to run, or they don't know that they should run away. They think they did something wrong and deserve to be treated that way."

"Will she really be all right with your father?"

Matilda nodded. "My father has a temper and I've seen that anger on a few occasions, but I can't imagine him hurting Abigail. Besides if he ever does, I'll come for her and take her away. My pa was stressed raising us, working long hours and coming home to less than perfect circumstances. I didn't know how to cook because no one showed me. I could only make a few things." She grinned at Beatrice. "I wouldn't be surprised to see my dad build her a house. After all, how many men his age have the chance to start over with a new wife?"

Quite a few of the townspeople gathered at the church to see Abigail marry. She looked so pretty in her empire-style, yellow dress and the flowers that she carried went perfectly with it.

Matilda wasn't certain where her father found the wedding band for Abigail, but Matilda had the feeling it had once belonged to her mother.

Abigail smiled so brightly through the whole church service that Matilda decided that no one could be happier at a wedding than the bride herself. Then afterwards, everyone went to the boardinghouse for coffee and cake. Someone was passing around a flask of alcohol among the men, but the groom seemed to be staying sober. Actually he stayed by Abigail's side, often with his arm around her waist. Matilda knew her father was happier than he'd been in years.

I wonder what you'll think when you discover your bride is with child? Or do you suspect?

Zeke watched the wedding preparations happening around him. Mrs. Haas was excited and kept adding more items to the menu until Cook put her foot down and said no. The house was cleaned from top to bottom as they prepared for company. Even the living quarters in the barn and the bunkhouse were scrubbed clean.

Mr. Haas made certain that Zeke had a suit for the wedding. And then schooled Zeke on his social skills.

The wedding was to take place outside in Mrs. Haas' garden, which was a riot of colors. After Cook complained, Mr. Haas hired several people from Hanover to help prepare everything. Then she complained that she couldn't do her own work because she was too busy overseeing everyone else.

Zeke couldn't help laughing at some of what was happening. He and Clay tried hard to stay out of sight and away from the house. But when Wednesday came, Zeke was ready to find Mattie and make her his woman.

He rode off early in the wee hours of the morning, taking Shep and the new puppy, Tricks, with him.

It was early evening when he arrived in Homestead Canyon. And short of standing in the middle of town and calling her name, he went to the boardinghouse, hoping he'd be able to buy something to eat. He knocked on the door and waited.

A woman with the prettiest smile and face answered the door. "Hello, may I help you?"

"I'm in town to pick up Mattie Berwyn, but I could use a meal."

"You mean Matilda?"

He nodded.

"Well. Supper was a few hours ago, but let me see what I can find for you."

He nodded and followed the woman inside. "Do you know where Mattie is?"

"Most likely, she's getting ready for bed."

"She's here?"

"Of course. Did you expect her to impose on friends for an entire week?"

"Please tell her I'm here."

The woman looked at him as though he had bean vines growing from each ear. "Have a seat."

She charged him three cents and left him with a plate of cold food and a cup of coffee.

Noise of someone entering the kitchen caused him to look up. "Mattie!"

She smiled and came to him. "Oh, Zeke, there's so much I want to tell you, but not now."

"Would you consider taking a walk?"

"I'm in my robe and nightgown."

"You look lovely to me and quite covered." He stuffed the

last piece of food into his mouth and motioned for her to follow.

"What's wrong? Why are you limping?"

He gave her his best grin. "It's only when I'm tired. Remember when I told you I broke my leg?" He rolled up his pants' leg. "Two surgeries."

"Does it still hurt?"

"No. I'm fine. For whatever reason, when I'm tired, I tend to limp."

"You didn't tell me about the surgeries."

"I was trying not to worry you. And don't worry about me now. The leg is strong." He took her hand in his. "That bull was instrumental in my decision to raise sheep instead of cattle."

"Are you certain your leg is strong?"

"I'm not a cripple. I can protect you, Mattie."

Matilda sat on the steps of the meetinghouse and told Zeke about her father's wedding, her party at Rosalind's, and the telegram. "I'm so sorry I doubted you."

"Maybe we've both learned a lesson. The next time something comes up, we know that it's important that we discuss it without coming to premature conclusions." He took her hand in his. "I want my wife to be independent, yet still be very much my wife. I don't want to you feel as though I will do all the thinking. We can work on things together."

"I see so much of that here, I mean the part about the men thinking for the women. It's as though women aren't allowed to have their own thoughts." She squeezed his hand. "Maybe because everyone thought I was a boy, I was allowed to think on my own. Around here, women do as their husbands or fathers say, even your mother and sisters are like that. I think I drove your father crazy."

"I'll never hold you to the concept that I know what is best. There's nothing wrong with your brains. You are quite capable of making your own decisions." He smiled broadly. "I like your independence. I don't think I could cope with a woman who hung on me for every move she made."

"Does that mean I don't have to ask your permission to have a friend spend the night?"

"Why would you need to do that?"

"I don't know, but Lena asked her husband if I could spend a few days with her."

"And he turned you down?"

"Oh, no. I spent two nights there until there was room for me at the boardinghouse. But I thought it was odd that she had to ask permission."

"That's something minor."

"Maybe if it is something major, we should discuss it."

"That's reasonable." He pursed his lips. "I think I should tell you that the Haases are planning on giving us a big wedding when we return. They sent for the pastor of a church in Gilmore, to officiate. And they've been sending invitations to people they know."

"Oh."

"That's the way I feel about it."

Zeke waited patiently while Mattie said goodbye to all her friends. She had dressed in a plain dress that reminded him of the dirndls that he saw some of the German women wearing in Germantown. Hers was plainer but showed off her natural curves.

The woman at the boardinghouse had packed them plenty of food. He loaded Mattie's trunk on a small cart that he pulled behind his horse. Then he crossed his fingers that Mattie could ride for hours. It didn't take him long to discover that Mattie had never really learned to ride a horse. They often stopped and walked. What should have taken one long day became two long days.

Sleeping in the open was new to Mattie and she was a little fearful, but he promised with Shep nearby, he'd keep an eye out for any problems that might arise. Somehow Zeke managed to sleep with Mattie in his arms even though his desire burned within him. *In a few more days, she'll be mine.*

They arrived at the Haas' home late at night. Mattie didn't want to keep going, but he promised it wasn't much further.

Cook took her to a room in the house while Zeke went to his room in the barn. Sleeping with her had been difficult, but sleeping without her was twice as grueling.

Morning broke, and as the light filtered into Zeke's room, he jumped to his feet. He made his way to the kitchen where Cook was fixing breakfast.

"Top of the morn!" Cook's cheery greeting was more than he was ready to handle.

"Coffee?"

"As if you have to ask me where you will find it? Didn't you sleep?"

"Not much. Too much on my mind."

"I'd say it's that lass on your mind."

He grinned as he poured a cup of coffee. "Yes. I wasn't counting sheep."

She shook her head. "You only have a few more days. You can wait that long."

"I worry about what they are planning."

"A wedding. All you have to do is show up looking your best and smelling like you've been rolling in the flowers."

"I'll do whatever it takes to marry Mattie."

"You found yourself a pretty little lass, and she certainly is tiny."

"I know. That worries me – babies and all that."

Cook tittered with her delicate bird-like giggle. "Women are made to have babies. Just keep what you have to yourself and don't expect her to be making a bairn every year or two. Talk to Clay."

Zeke knew, for his father had told him several things he could do to prevent a child.

He ate his breakfast and began the morning chores. *I hope this goes well for Mattie.*

Matilda awakened in the prettiest room she'd ever seen. Quickly she prepared for the day and wondered who these people were.

A little girl knocked on her bedroom door. "Guten Morgen, I am Phyllis. It is time for breakfast."

"Good Morning to you. My name is Matilda."

The child scrunched her nose. "Zeke said your name is Mattie."

"That's what he calls me, but it's really Matilda."

"Oh." She looked around the bedroom as if searching for something. "Are you going to marry Zeke?"

"Yes."

She frowned. "I don't want him to go away. He takes me for pony rides."

"Then I know you will miss him, but you can write to him. That way he'll never really be gone."

"Will he write back?"

It was all Matilda could do to keep from laughing. "Yes. I will make certain that he answers your letters."

It started with breakfast that morning and continued over the next few days with a flurry of preparations for her wedding. Her dress was pressed and made ready. Then the guests began to arrive.

The day before the wedding, she almost squealed when John and Lena Thorpe arrived with their son Robert, and right behind them was Rosalind, her husband Peter Van Dyke, and their son. But taking up the rear was her father and Abigail.

Matilda greeted everyone, but when she hugged her father, she could feel the tears welling in her eyes. "Pa, Abigail, I had no idea you'd be coming. This is all such a huge surprise." She swiped at the tears rolling down her cheeks. "I'm so happy you came."

Matilda couldn't hold back the tears of joy over seeing so many of her friends who made the long trip to attend her wedding.

There were other people the Haases invited that Matilda did not know, but they came for the wedding. And everyone brought gifts for the bride and groom.

And when the day came, Matilda discovered that she was nervous. She wanted to talk to Zeke, but he wasn't around. Her breakfast was served in her room, but she didn't feel at all hungry.

Lena knocked on her door. "May I help the bride?"

"Oh, Lena, I'm so happy to see you. What's happening? I was told I must stay here until it is time."

"We had the most marvelous breakfast. This place is unreal. John told me the Haases were wealthy, but I wasn't expecting this. I've only been in a few places in New Orleans that are as lovely as this house." She walked over to the breakfast tray. "Why didn't you eat?"

"Because my stomach is fluttering."

"At least, drink some tea and have one of these little rolls. The orange marmalade on them is delicious."

Matilda managed to drink her tea, but she didn't think anything more would stay in her stomach.

"Is this your dress? It's beautiful."

"Thank you. I bought it especially for my wedding."

Cook knocked on Matilda's door. "Your bath is ready. Do

not waste time!"

Matilda did as instructed and when she returned to her room, Lena was waiting with all sorts of lotions. She used something in Matilda's hair and then pulled it up in a fashionable style with fancy combs.

Once Matilda's hair was done, Lena dabbed some color on Matilda's cheeks, eyes, and lips before brushing powder on her face. She looked in the mirror and decided she didn't look so plain nor did she look like a tart.

After that, she ducked behind a screen, took off her robe and pulled on her undergarments. Lena then helped with the corset.

"Oh, please, I need to breathe."

"But it's your wedding day and you want to look extra special."

"I don't care. I need to breathe."

"If you insist, I'll loosen the ties."

There was a small knock on the door and Lena answered it.

"This is for Mattie. Cook said she is to have it for her hair."

"Thank you, Phyllis," Matilda called.

"May I come in?"

Lena answered before Matilda could. "No one is allowed to see the bride until the wedding."

"But you see her."

"Because I'm helping her to prepare. Thank you for the flowers and tell Cook thank you." Lena closed the door and returned to Matilda. "These flowers are beautiful. And why do they call her Cook? That is disrespectful."

"Zeke told me it is because no one can pronounce her first

name. I think it is Scottish or Welsh. He's heard Clay, that's her husband, calls her by her real name, but no one else does."

"Yes, but to be polite it should be Mrs. and then her last name."

"All I know is that she prefers to be called Cook."

Lena shook her head. "Lets put this on you." Lena fitted the crown of flowers on Matilda's head. "This is so pretty and it goes perfectly with your dress."

"I have a hat that matches."

"No hat. This is total perfection. Save the hat for another time."

Matilda walked over to the window and looked below as everyone gathered for the wedding. The wait seemed to take forever.

"Sit and relax," Lena fussed, as she checked her reflection in the large mirror.

"I can't sit. There's no sit left in me. I never was very good at doing nothing."

"You are so funny! Promise me you'll always write and that we'll always be friends!"

"Oh, I will. I do promise." Matilda smiled at Lena but her thoughts were with Zeke's family who were so far away. She was certain that they had been invited, but with a farm… She knew they couldn't leave when animals depended on them. *The same will happen to us.*

Finally there was a knock and it was Cook dressed in a black and white dress with a fancy white apron. "It is time. Here are more flowers for you to hold. It gives you something to do with your hands. Looking lovely, Mattie."

Matilda walked through the quiet house, and then outside to the garden. She almost didn't recognize Clay dressed up and playing the violin. But when she saw Zeke everything else faded away. He looked so handsome, and she was proud to marry him. She barely heard what the minister was saying, and when Zeke slipped the gold band on her hand, she could barely believe her eyes. Tiny golden-yellow stones that sparkled were set in the gold band.

Afterwards there was food, dancing, more food, and more partying. Zeke pulled her away and took her into the barn and to the room where he stayed. There she discovered her nightgown, robe, slippers, and everything she would need for morning.

"What? Who did this?"

Zeke laughed. "Cook. I wanted you out here where we'd be alone. She and Clay are going to take your room, so no one will suspect what we've done."

Her stomach developed butterflies as Zeke took her into his arms. This was the moment she'd been dreaming of and it was happening. His lips touched hers and she thought that she would melt. His fingers fumbled with all the buttons down the back of her dress. Then his lips traveled across her cheek, down her neck and over her shoulder. Eventually she faced away from him and his lips were on her back. She could feel his fingers on the buttons until the dress slid to the floor.

"How do I remove this contraption?"

She couldn't stop her giggle. "Undo the ties."

When that fell away, she stood feeling vulnerable in her lily-white underclothes. But the look on Zeke's face made her smile for he looked at her as though she were a delectable piece of fruit. She began to unbutton his shirt and exposed his chest. A patch of dark blond hair covered the center of his chest.

She sucked in a breath and then started on his pants. They fell to his ankles, where they caught on his boots.

He laughed as he waddled his way to his bed. "I think we did this wrong. Remind me to remove the footwear first." He pulled off his boots and pants, and then patted the spot beside him. "Come here. I see I have more buttons. Why must women's clothes be so complicated?"

She sat beside him. He dropped in front of her, slowly managing to remove her shoes before peeling her stockings off. The touch of his fingers against her skin tingled. Then he pulled her to her feet.

He slipped his underpants off and grinned.

"Oh." She knew but she didn't know. This wasn't a vague glimpse. The butterflies that she'd been feeling seemed to have taken flight in her stomach. But before she could say or do more her under things were removed.

"You are beautiful and you are mine. I've waited more than a year for this moment."

Her body quivered. "I have, too."

He wrapped his arms around her and she knew she wanted this. Some of the butterflies flew into her chest and made her heart skip a few beats. The others flew to that low spot and danced with anticipation. For the first time in her life, she knew what it was to love and to be loved.

Light streamed into the bedroom and Matilda looked at the man lying beside her as she raised her arms over her head and stretched. The signs of their coupling were evident and she wasn't exactly certain what she should do, but Zeke was as marked as she. She ran her fingers over his jaw line and his eyes fluttered open.

"Good morning." His voice was raspy as he pulled her on top of him. "What a wonderful way to awaken."

When they finally scurried from the bed, he showed her where the toilet was. Then she looked at the big, deep soapstone sink and stepped in it. The water was cool, but it felt refreshing as she bathed.

"Now that is a sight!" Zeke laughed. "I wish I fit in the sink."

She shrugged and stepped out. Quickly she dressed in her dark green dress that was left for her. It didn't have a bustle but it did have a slight poof with a big bow, giving it a very casual but still fashionable look.

Breakfast was a buffet served in the dining room. It appeared as though quite a few of the guests had slept in after their evening of drinking and partying. But most were leaving after they had eaten. Matilda's father hugged and kissed her, wishing her much luck. Abigail wound up in tears and thanked Matilda for everything she had done.

Rosalind and Lena also dissolved into tears, and they promised to write. Matilda held Robert. She tickled his tummy and kissed his chubby cheeks. "Someday I'll have my own little boy."

"You will. He's so much fun."

Rosalind laughed. "Babies are also work. But a year from now, you'll have your own little one."

Matilda raised her eyebrows. "Maybe. We have a mountain of things to do before I need to think about having a child."

Lena laughed. "One year, that's all you'll have."

"Zeke and I have talked about it. We're going to try to prevent that from happening until we have the ranch on its feet."

"How?" Rosalind asked.

Matilda could feel the heat rising to her cheeks. "Ask Jolene or Ruby."

"I couldn't do that." Rosalind put her hand to her chest. "Please tell us."

Matilda looked around and then whispered, "Two things. And remember nothing works completely. It can be covered with a sheath, but I've heard it is not the best way. Or the man withdraws before you know… before."

Lena giggled. "It's very messy."

"You know about such things?" Rosalind's eyes grew wide.

Lena nodded. "I thought all women knew."

Matilda giggled. "Zeke's mother told me, and she had nine children."

Lena laughed. "Zeke's dad had lousy timing or she hated washing the sheets."

Abigail came to where they were all standing. "The men are waiting."

"Oh, dear. I guess we must leave."

Another round of hugs and Matilda waved goodbye to her

family and friends. It was Zeke's arm she felt, slipping around her waist as he stood next to her. She leaned against him, grateful to have him by her side.

When the train came through, several more people left and a few others were leaving the following morning.

"It's up to you, we can leave today and ride for a few hours or we can leave early tomorrow morning."

Matilda looked up. "If we leave tonight, will it give us a head start?"

"It's not a leisurely ride. Are you going to be able to do it?"

She nodded. "How difficult is it to sit in a saddle? I made it here didn't I?"

"The way we will travel, it will take about ten days."

"It didn't take me that long to come up here."

"That's because you were on a coach that switched horses and drivers so that it could go almost non-stop. We will have to stop. If I take a cart, it will slow us down more."

She smiled at her handsome husband. "I can ride. I'm strong."

"Then we'll leave in the morning. I think you've been through enough today."

That night they said their goodbyes to the Haases. Zeke and Matilda planned to head out as dawn began to break. To lighten the load, Matilda's trunk was being shipped, and she only kept a few basic necessities with her.

Cook packed some provisions, in case they had a problem along the way. But they managed to roll everything and not have to take the cart with them.

By the time they tumbled into Zeke's bed, they were exhausted. Matilda mumbled, "I'm so glad we decided to wait until morning."

"Yes, this will be better." Zeke wrapped his arms around her and fell asleep.

She snuggled tight to him and breathed in his natural scent. Her eyes closed as she memorized the sensation of his protective embrace. Then she struggled to open her eyes. It was still dark as Zeke slid from the bed.

He showed her how to saddle her horse, before helping her into the saddle. She didn't feel awake or ready to face the new day. Shep and Tricks circled them as they began their long ride.

The first thing Zeke did was buy her cowboy boots in Hanover. "You need them. Your foot will rest better in the stirrup, and if for some reason you fall off, your foot will slide free of the boot. That way you won't be dragged."

She scrunched up her nose, but when she saw the pretty boots, she decided they weren't so terrible.

Zeke also bought her a hat with a large brim to protect her face and neck.

They stopped in small towns and ate. And they stopped in a few bigger ones and spent the night in a hotel. As they left the small hotel in Sheridan, Matilda did not want to admit that she didn't think she'd manage another day in the saddle.

After about an hour, she thought maybe she'd scream. "Zeke, I can't do it. I can't go on."

Zeke reined in and dismounted. "Okay, we can walk, but

we're not that far and we should be there tonight."

"I can't. I don't think I can even walk. It's my back. I hurt to my knees."

He lifted her from her horse. "Okay, we can rest."

She sat on the ground and then moved so she was on her side.

"Mattie, darling, you have blood on your skirt."

Tears flowed from the corners of her eyes. "It's too soon. I'm not prepared."

"Tell me how I can help?"

She shook her head. "I'm so embarrassed."

He leaned over her and kissed her cheek. "I am your husband. I know about women. What do you need?"

Zeke convinced her that she had to move from where she was. There was a gully where they could spend the night and not be seen from the road. She made it to the gully and managed to change her clothes.

As darkness was starting to settle, she saw Indians and nudged Zeke. "Do you think they are Sioux?"

Zeke said a quick prayer. "I have no idea."

Mattie called to the men and said something that he did not understand. Three of the men rode to them. Whatever the conversation was he didn't understand a word of it.

One Indian dismounted and came to where she was sitting. She smiled and the Indian looked concerned.

Mattie asked, "Do we have any food left?"

"A jar of beans, that's our dinner or breakfast. I suggest that you don't give it to them or we'll be very hungry."

"Give them the beans and trust me."

Zeke didn't like what was happening, but he did as Mattie asked. She leaned against him and he wrapped his arms around her.

As the sun began to set, the Indian returned. He handed them each a piece of cornbread and a gourd bowl. Zeke could tell that traces of his beans were in the bowl, but there was also meat.

Mattie dipped her forefinger and middle finger into the bowl and scooped some of the meat. "Rabbit. It's delicious."

He did what she did and ate his bowl of food. When she was done, she handed the man her bowl so Zeke did the same.

She looked at Zeke and smiled. "They will watch over us and keep us safe tonight."

Zeke must have closed his eyes because a gunshot startled him awake. It didn't take him long to decipher that the Indians had killed a male wolf.

"Zeke, there are two of us and plenty of them. My… a woman… at this time, it is much like an animal in heat. I'm very attractive to the wildlife." Mattie giggled. "The Indians are more than happy to watch over me. I am bait."

"Well, I don't need a wolf roaming these parts. They like sheep." He kissed her forehead. "How are you feeling?"

"Not as bad as yesterday. I've never experienced such pain."

"You've also never ridden as you have these last few days."

She furrowed her brow. "Do you want to ride or sleep a

little more?"

"I don't think there's any sleep left in me knowing there was a wolf out there."

She smiled at him. "I want to go to our new home."

He helped Mattie to her feet and he assumed she said goodbye to the men as she climbed into the saddle. She rubbed her lower back and forced a smile.

He put his foot in a stirrup and swung into the saddle. "It's still a long ride."

"I'm ready."

He didn't want to think about how hungry he was, but he reminded himself that there was ample food when he reached the house.

Somehow they managed to approach the house before the sun set, even though they walked a fair part of the time instead of riding.

"Ruth!" Zeke called as he pulled in front of the house. "Ruth!"

Ruth came around the side of the house. "You made it. I was wondering if you were ever going to return."

"Ruth, meet my wife Mattie." He turned to his wife and helped her down. "Mattie, this is my oldest sister who I hope has supper ready for us because we haven't eaten much in the last forty-eight hours."

"I get the hint. See you inside." Ruth stomped back to the kitchen.

Once inside, he led Mattie to a door. "Your library. It only has one small bookshelf, but I don't see any books yet."

"A real library for me? And you built it?"

"I want my wife to be happy."

She smiled at him. "I need to tell you something… Oh, I can see you still have lots of work to do. I think I'll have to buy some boys clothes so that I can help, because I can't be using a saw or hammer in a dress." She threw her arms around his neck. "Remember when you thought I was panning for gold?"

"Yes."

"I was and it was more than a tiny nugget. I found quite a few nuggets, some the size of my palm."

"Something like that is worth a fortune."

"I know. I exchanged it for cash on my way to your parents. Not all of it, I kept a few pieces. But I have plenty of money for us. I also gave my father enough to build a house for him and Abigail."

"Does your father know you killed Abigail's husband?"

"No. I was dealing with some guilt until I saw my father with Abigail. That's when I realized I'd done them both a huge favor. Abigail's front teeth are chipped because of that horrible man, and my father has quit drinking and is happy. Abigail has never had children and now she's with child."

"Is that why your father married her?"

"My father married her because he loves her. She apparently hadn't told him about her condition. He'll figure it out eventually."

Zeke pressed his lips to Mattie's.

Ruth hollered. "You told me you were starving. Are you going to come eat?"

Mattie looked up at Zeke. "Oh, I'm starving for my new life as Ezekiel Hillerman's wife."

"Then you've come to the right place, because I can't imagine sharing my life with anyone but you. I love you, my darling Mattie."

"I love you, too."

THE END

NEW RELEASE

Find your favorite romance novels at

Indie Artist Press!

www.indieartistpress.com

NEW RELEASE

DOWNLOAD
TODAY!

Find your favorite romance novels at

Indie Artist Press!

www.indieartistpress.com

Did you enjoy reading *Loving Matilda*
by E. Ayers?

If you did, please consider leaving a review of the book on your favorite venue. You can write to the author directly at her website.

http://www.ayersbooks.com/

ABOUT THE AUTHOR

Born and raised in Pennsylvania not far from Philadelphia and very close to her forefathers' lands, Elizabeth Ayers grew up with a strong sense of heritage. A tomboy, she was usually found on the back of a horse and not always in proper English attire. She knew every creek and pond, swam in plenty, and learned never to let your feet touch the bottom of the pond if it was shared with ducks.

Her family loved to travel and she can tell you where she hasn't been easier than she can tell you where she has been. Before she married, she'd logged thousands of air miles and even lived through an emergency landing in a large commercial jet with no landing gear. She swears it was the noisiest landing ever but also the smoothest.

As a teen, she moved to a small island in the Atlantic Ocean and while living there she met her husband. He swore the minute he saw her he knew he'd marry her. She claims it took a whole evening of chatting over cheese steaks before she realized she had fallen in love. He was twenty-four and she was seven years younger. He never asked how old she was and she never volunteered her age. It wasn't until the subject of marriage came up that he discovered that she was underage. The day she turned eighteen, they got their marriage license, and a few days later, they were married. They'd known each other less than five weeks.

With two years of college credits under her belt, she'd laugh and say she wasn't the normal teen. Before her nineteenth birthday, they had moved to Virginia, bought a brand new house, had two cars in the driveway, and a newborn. It might have sounded exciting, but it was actually a rather quiet life. She gardened organically, and spent most of her days learning new domestic skills.

She and her husband had two girls. It didn't take her long to realize that her girls were running out of reading material. They were both good readers but not ready for the more adult stories, so she began to write stories for them. Then she got serious and figured she'd have her stories published. A friend's daughter was a New York best seller and she did a little arm-twisting and convinced Elizabeth to put aside children's stories in favor of romances. Elizabeth said she hated romances because they weren't real. That author said to write them the way should be told. Elizabeth thought about it and said okay.

Her husband never lived long enough to see her first book

published, but he was her cheering squad as she began her writing career. His constant faith in her pushed her forward and kept her writing. His unexpected death forced her decide if writing was what she really wanted to do. She swears that was the easiest choice she'd ever made and thousands of readers agree.

Life is still just as quiet. Living in an antebellum home means that it's rare that everything works as it should. Her honey-do list became her impossible to do list. And if things get a little too quiet, the ghosts remind her that they lived in the house first.

Additional Books by E. Ayers

A Snowy Christmas in Wyoming (a novella)
A Cowboy's Kiss in Wyoming (a novella)
A Love Song in Wyoming (a novella)
A Calling in Wyoming (a novella)
Baby It's Cold Outside (a collection of novellas)

A Rancher's Woman (a historical novel)
A Rancher's Dream (a historical novel)
A Rancher's Request (a historical novel)
Loving Ellen (a historical novella)
Loving Arabelle (a historical novella)
Sweetwater Springs Christmas (a historical anthology)

Indie Artist Press | Brackettville, Texas